Outrunners - First Days

A collection of short stories

By David Noë

Huge thanks to Karl Relf for the research and feedback he provided.
https://karlrelf.wordpress.com/

Extensive feedback was also provided by Vanessa G. I don't think I could have done this without your encouragement and enthusiasm, thank you.

To all my friends at ChaosNova, thank you for helping me keep the writing dream alive.
http://chaosnova.co.uk/

And finally, thank you to my parents for all the support they've provided over the years.

- Cataclysm
- Solution
- Gathering
- Reality
- Another
- Storm
- Project
- Surface

1. Cataclysm - Katie Carter

"...Nineteen fifty-two, the government took twenty-five acres from a local family and built this bunker. It was active all the way up until nineteen ninety-four."

Katie fought back a yawn as she scribbled the details down. She could barely hear the guide over the whispered conversations of other visitors as he led them farther down a well-lit corridor.

"This tunnel is a hundred and twenty yards long and leads to the bunker proper. Hundreds of people would have used this in the event of a nuclear attack or another such catastrophe. Thankfully, that was never the case."

"Obviously…" She whispered under her breath.

"Of course, you'd need a bunker like this to protect you from more than just fallout. Society would break down, people would become desperate, and since Kelvedon was supplied to feed six-hundred people for three months, you can see why it would be an appealing target. Then there's always the potential of an invading force. Lots of things to consider when building a place like this."

As Katie tried to mute the growing irritation she felt from the guides ramblings, someone near the front of the group asked a question she didn't quite hear.

"Oh, I wouldn't know about that. My focus is here, at Kelvedon. You'd need to ask someone from the government about new builds, but I wouldn't hold on for an answer. The point of these places is to remain secret. The public doesn't find out about them until they're decommissioned."

Another murmur from the front followed by some laughter.

"Yes." The guide snorted. "But then I think it's better to have them and not need them over the alternative."

The group bunched up to squeeze by several metal beds hanging from the wall on chains. Katie snagged her jacket on the bundle of wires running the length of the corridor. She sighed, unhooked herself, and then hurried to catch up.

"...Blast doors each weigh about a tonne and a half." He motioned for everyone to step through, and then followed after them, pulling the door shut. He swung the arm down and turned to the group. "Once they're shut, people would be able to survive down here for three months without going outside."

Katie glanced around at the thick, textured walls. She caught a slight hint of staleness in the air, an old smell, like a long-forgotten building falling to dust. In one corner, two grey boxes stood out in the otherwise featureless corridor. She studied the many dials and meters poking out from behind a 'Danger Do Not Touch' sign.

"If you'd like to come this way." The guide continued as he led the group around the corner. "The bunker is spread across three levels, and the-" He paused, his eyes darted about as if looking for something. "Hmm. Sorry. As I was saying, the bunker is spread across three levels, and the room we're heading to now is known as the-"
The floor beneath them made a slight movement. Then another.

Katie hurriedly stuffed her pen into her coat and steadied herself against the wall. The movements grew stronger, more violent. People crashed into one another, then to the floor. She turned to see a tall man slam into the door with a loud thud. He looked at her with a blank expression, and then fell forward.

It was over in a matter of seconds, but the damage had been done. Those gathered glanced cautiously between one another, then slowly got to their feet.

Katie moved over to the door and tried to rouse the man, now passed out in an uncomfortable looking bundle on the floor. "I need some help over here!"

Most of the group just looked to one another with blank stares or were trying to get their bearings. Katie could overhear the desperation in their voices, asking things like "Is it safe now?" and "Was that an earthquake?"

The guide was in a trance, wondering around unsure of what to do. A man with a thick, dark-brown beard pushed through them and crouched opposite Katie.

"Harry."

"Katie."

"How can I help?"

"You know first aid?"

"Some." He nodded to the guide. "Our host here should know

what to do, public building and all that."

Katie shot a look at the guide. "Unless you can get him to focus, he's not much help."

"Then I guess it's on us." Harry took his jacket off and rolled it up, placing it under the man's head. He let out a pained moan. Katie tried to keep him awake. "Hey. I need you to keep talking to me, okay?"

"Uhh?"

"You banged your head. Some kind of quake. What's your name?"

"A-Aiden."

"Good. You remember what day it is?"

"Uhh… Friday?"

"Yeah. What about a date?"

"The… Er, Twenty-first of May?"

Harry nodded. "I think he'll be fine. Question is, what do we do?"

Katie looked over at the other people gathered; all of them had a lost look in their eyes. "Not sure…" She shrugged. "Don't find myself in these situations often. We should probably call an ambulance; I think people need checking over."

"We'll need to go back to the entrance," Harry replied, shaking his phone in her direction. "No signal."

As he rose to his feet, Katie pulled hers out and tapped the screen. "Emergency calls only. Good enough, lemme…" She dialed the numbers and put the phone to her ear. After a few seconds, she blinked, and then looked to Harry with confusion. "It's… engaged?"

"Probably a lot of people trying to get through. I'll head to the entrance, try and find help."

"I'll stay here. Make sure everyone's okay."

Harry tugged at the bar holding the door shut. It didn't budge. "Tonne and a half of door and the thing jams? You're kidding me."

Katie's face flushed white. "We're trapped in here?"

"I guess so…" He turned back to her, wearing a frown of concentration. "Since that's the case, maybe we should move everyone out of this corridor? And maybe slap some sense into the caretaker. This can't be the only way out."

Katie took a deep breath, stood up and nudged through the group until she came face to face with the guide. He was sitting in a plastic chair, mumbling to himself.

"Hey. Hey, it's over now. Besides a few bumps and scrapes,

everybody's fine. Little earthquake, heck, we might even be able to continue the tour."

He raised his head and looked at her, glassy-eyed. "Have we been hit?"

"Hit?" Katie scrunched her nose. "What are you talking about? You mean like… bombed?"

Harry wandered up beside her. "I hadn't considered that. Haven't been in enough quakes or explosions to know the difference." He blew the air out of his cheeks. "This potentially changes things. But who'd wanna bomb the U.K?"

"Okay look." Katie raised a finger. "All this speculation is ridiculous, and the way most of you are acting is… Ugh. We're all adults, right? Let's start behaving like it. All we know, a little rumble just shook this bunker some. It isn't a big deal, and we're probably in the safest place we can be if it was an earthquake. Let's pick our jaws up off the floor, and find somewhere to calm down until we know what's happening." She helped the guide to his feet. "And no more theories. It just makes people anxious."

"I don't think you understand-"

Harry nudged him on the shoulder. "It's alright. If I spent all my time in a bunker, I'd probably assume the same, she's right though, we don't know anything yet."

He drew breath to reply, but Katie fixed him with an expectant glare. He straightened up, exhaled, and continued down the corridor.

Harry helped Aiden to his feet, made sure he could walk, reclaimed his jacket, then caught up with Katie. He spoke in hushed tones. "I know things are tense, but you should go easier on them."

"I shouldn't be doing anything. Yeah, fair enough, none of us expected this. But when it happened I wasn't expecting everyone to fall to pieces, or stand about like lemons. I dunno. Thought us Brits were made of sterner stuff."

"I don't think it was what happened, more the not knowing. Maybe shock too. Like you said, never thought something like this would happen. Caught us all off guard."

"Until Aiden smashed into the door, I honestly thought it was part of the tour. You know, like interactive. 'Oh no, something has happened, and now you get to experience life as one of the lucky survivors!'" She sighed. "I hate that stuff. Just want the information, don't wanna be part of an 'experience'."

"What do you do?"

"For a living?" Katie's eyes thinned. "I'm a student."

"Oh? University I take it?"

"Yeah…" She replied, nodding as best she could while walking. "Studying journalism. Supposed to be doing a piece on a hypothetical World War Three. That's why I'm here."

"In a Cold War bunker?"

"Yeah. Remarkably they haven't made any new ones public, so this is a good as it gets. Been to Hack Green too. That's probably as modern as I'm gonna find. Unless war does actually break out and we're ushered into some previously classified location."

Harry drew breath to reply, then paused and fell quiet. They walked the rest of the way in silence.

They emerged into a room Katie immediately recognized. Tables ran the length, in the far corner, the tell-tale glowing lights and bare metal of a serving area.

"Okay, good. This canteen is a perfect place to settle while we figure out what's happened."

The tour guide grunted. "Mess-hall."

"Yeah…" She replied under her breath. "Like it matters…"

She let her mind settle, then addressed the room. "Alright

everyone, get comfortable, we're going to try and find help."

The small group ebbed around her. Katie looked back to the guide. "I couldn't hear you earlier when you introduced yourself?"

"Edward Allens, Kelvedon Hatch preserve-"

"I'm Katie, this is Harry. The main door jammed, is there another way out?"

"Hmph. Well… of course there is. We had to have a way for the fire brigade to get into the bunker."

"Can you show us?"

"What about all these people?"

Harry nodded. "He's right."

Katie rubbed her forehead. "Alright. How about… You point us towards the exit, we use our phones to get help, then once help gets here, we guide them back here."

"Why me?"

Harry grinned. "You're the tour guide. It's your job to look after folk. Let the spry, young people do all the running about."

"It's exactly that reason that I should be guiding you through this recognized historic landmark! I know the way! You might damage something!"

"I think the quake already took care of that," Harry replied, glancing back to the group as they scooped chairs up off the floor and sat down.

"If they all stay here, and don't touch anything-"

"Alright!" Katie threw her arms up. "For Pete's sake, just go already!"

As he begrudgingly stepped between them, Harry looked to Katie, palms up. "Easy."

She rolled her eyes and fell in behind Edward. "You're not helping."

"I get it, stressful situation. But we're doing everything we can, right? No sense getting worked up over something that's already happened."

"Look, you might be speaking all the sense in the world, but it isn't… I can't process it, alright? It'll take me some time to calm down, and then I'll be open to… 'external contributions'. Not right now. Even vocalizing this has taken a lot of my energy, so just leave it, alright?"

Harry raised his hands again, this time defensively. "Got it."

Edward led them through several rooms, and up a flight of

stairs. As they reached the top, he stopped and glanced to the floor.

"Hmm?"

"What?" Katie replied, then paused and followed his eye line. "Oh. Water? Does your bomb-proof bunker often flood?"

Edward shook his head. "This is going to cause untold damage!"

Harry looked down the corridor. "Where's it coming from?"

"No doubt that wretched access door!"

Katie pushed by him and trudged down the corridor cautiously. "So we follow the water?"

"Unless that quake knocked a pipe loose or something, I'd say so."

Edward mumbled. "You're almost there. I have to go find the pump. Try not to cause any more damage, thank you."

"He's saying it like it's our fault."

Katie didn't reply, the moisture seeping into her boots was causing some discomfort. She was roused from her thoughts by a loud banging from farther ahead. "What's that?"

Harry shrugged. "No idea. Maybe it was a loose pipe? Banging against something?"

"No… it's… like a police knock."

Harry sped up slightly. "We should probably go let them in then."

Katie turned the corner and saw Harry trying to open a door with a familiar green logo above it.

"This one's jammed shut too!" He gave it a knock. "Hello?"

"At least we know where the water's coming from-" She was startled by a bang. "Jesus!"

"Let me in!"

"It's jammed!"

"Is it unlocked?"

"Just unlocked it! Still won't budge!"

"Stand back!"

Harry almost stumbled over himself as he stepped backward. There was a loud bang, then another. Katie jumped each time.

"Ugh... Aghh!"

The door swung open, slamming into the wall with another almighty crash before wobbling back on its hinges. Katie watched as a rain-drenched woman fell through the opening, bringing with her a small wave of water. A sledge-hammer wobbled in the flood behind her.

"What's going on?" Katie shouted over the torrential storm

outside.

Harry helped her to her feet, then poked his head out the door. It led out to a corrugated metal arch, which itself led to a final external doorway. Wind smashed against it, flashes of light filled the exit, and the roar of thunder seemed endless. Harry dragged the sledgehammer into the bunker and pushed the door shut. As the lock fell home, he let out a sigh of relief. "Thank you!"

Katie studied the woman leaning against the opposite wall, breathing heavily, then offered her a hand. "Katie. He's Harry."

"Reilly." She took the offered hand and gave it a half-assed shake. "Dunno how long I'd have lasted out there. Came out of nowhere."

"Did you feel the earthquake?" Katie asked, discreetly wiping the damp on her coat.

"Earthquake?" Reilly frowned and stood to full height. "Earthquake was the least of my worries. I was banging in a fence, next thing I know, the heavens opened, the wind kicked up something fierce too. I could barely move, instantly drenched through, constantly getting knocked over. I thought to myself 'Well this isn't normal'. Jumped in my truck and headed here. Thought a 'Secret Nuclear Bunker' would be happy to give me tea and shelter for a spell if I chucked 'em a few quid." She rubbed her forehead. "It died on me just shy of the entrance. Or, er, where the entrance used to be. Grabbed my hammer and ran for the back door."

Katie frowned. "What do you mean, used to be?"

"The bungalow? Where they sign the guests in?"

"Yeah?"

"Pile of rubble. Mostly. The wind tore the roof off right before my eyes. Need a new windscreen now too."

"Jesus…"

"Reckon it'll do the same to that flimsy tinfoil building out there given enough time. Think the plants are all that's holding it down."

Harry looked between the two of them. "This sounds bad. Really bad."

"You two been down here the whole time?"

"I guess so. Wasn't raining when we arrived." Harry stepped back. "Oh man. My car was parked up there."

Reilly shrugged. "Not anymore it ain't. Not unless you and everyone else decided to park in the trees. It's weird, you know? I always thought they had underground parking here…"

"This doesn't make any sense." Katie shook her head. "The weather forecast never said anything about rain... or storms... It was supposed to be a bit chilly, that's all." Her gaze fell on Harry. "Wait. This means we can't call for help."

Reilly frowned. "There's no help. Not locally anyway. I'm amazed I survived to be fair."

"So what do we do?"

Reilly pointed at the floor. "If I were you, I'd do something about this leak. Might be here for a few hours. Probably best not to spend the last few minutes of that swimming."

"You're pretty nonchalant about all this."

Reilly nodded. "Two minutes ago, I thought I was gonna die. If I had a piano, I'd immortalize you both in song."

"Oh. You play the piano?" Harry asked in a vague attempt to keep the conversation flowing.

"No, but I'd learn just to immortalize you both in song."

Katie shook her head. "Can we just plug this hole, please?"

"With what?"

"There's got to be something around here. What about those mattresses in the tunnel?"

"That's a long way from here, and I doubt they'd do the job for long."

Reilly shrugged out of her work jacket. "You got clothes, just jam them in." She pressed the thin waterproof into the gap at the bottom of the door, then looked to the others expectantly.

"I-" Katie exhaled, dug her notepad and pens out, handed them to Harry, then slinked out of her coat, reluctantly passing it to Reilly. "It's not like yours."

"Doesn't matter, as long as it makes water access more difficult." She stepped back and looked at her work. A mix of hi-viz and a dull red certainly added colour to the otherwise featureless door. "Reckon that'll do it."

Harry nodded. "I'll come up and check it every now and then, keep an eye out for this storm to pass too."

"Sounds good. So what's the plan? I assume we're not just gonna hang out here until then?"

"There's a ca- Sorry. There's a 'Mess-hall' downstairs."

Reilly grinned. "Alright. Lead on."

2. Solution - Rachel Starsy

"Rachel! Hey Rachel! Wake up!"

An arm stretched out from under a blanket of hoodies.

"Hnnnng. Damnit, Mo'. Keep the noise down."

"You told me to wake you up when the weather improved."

The pile of clothes moved again, then fell to the side as a figure emerged. Rachel sat up and rubbed her eyes. "It's over?"

"Yeah, people are trying to get the hatch open."

Rachel groaned and pulled herself up using the bare concrete wall. Once she was steady, she reached down and grabbed a hoodie from the pile. After brushing the dust off, she stretched into it and yawned again. "I'd kill for some coffee…"

"The first cafe we come across, drinks are on me."

"Let's hope they hold up better than this place…"

"We can certainly dream." Mohammed held the door open with a smile. "After you."

"Thanks."

The small box room was connected to a long concrete tunnel. Cracked white paint lined the lower half while pipework and wiring ran the length of the bare upper portion. Rachel carefully walked around a broken engine hoist, between the frames of old filing cabinets, and onto some scaffolding boards.

"Makes you wonder, doesn't it?"

Rachel looked back to Mohammed with curious eyes. "Oh?"

"What's going to happen to this place?"

"Anchor?" Rachel pointed to the wires. "It's an underground telephone exchange. Still in use."

"Really?" He motioned to the surrounding junk. "People work here?"

"Sure do. I'm only here because they wanted someone to check the wiring." She pointed at the ceiling. "I was hoping for a quick job. This place is riddled with asbestos."

Mohammed lifted his shirt over his mouth. "Really?"

"It's mostly sealed, just gotta be careful not to damage it."

Ascending the stairs, Rachel was glad to see the once crowded control room now mostly devoid of life besides the odd stragglers. They wandered between the desks, avoiding the mess of food wrappers and drinks cans littering the floor.

"So what's next for you, Mo?"

"Not sure. Probably go home, see what the damage is. Then I'm going to treat myself to a shower."

Rachel sighed. "Oh, that would be nice. I might go for a bath actually…" She gave her hands a cursory glance, her eyes darted over the spots of dust and dried paint flecks. "Shower first actually. Then a nice, hot, soothing bath."

"Well whatever you decide, I hope you enjoy it." He pulled open a door leading to another corridor, rooms lined either side. There were more people sorting through their belongings. "After that… I'll call work, see what the situation is."

"No family?"

"They're on holiday."

"Anywhere nice?"

Mohammed grinned. "Nicer than here. I imagine people were able to go outside on the beautiful island of Tenerife "

"Well, it was a bit of excitement I suppose… we were on a holiday of our own." She laughed. "I give it two stars. Awful food, no beds, and the service leave a lot to be desired."

Mo' exhaled, apparently oblivious of Rachel's attempt at humour. "I wonder what caused it… Haven't seen weather like that before."

"Who knows? I hope this isn't the result of climate change or something. If that's the case, I imagine that won't be our last 'weather hiccup'."

"How are we supposed to deal with something like that again?"

"No clue. More flood defenses, better warning systems? The government will probably set up a 'task force'. As long as it means I don't have to live underground for a weekend again, they can do whatever they want."

They reached a set of thick double doors at the end of the corridor. Rachel could hear shouting coming from the other side. Mo pulled one side open, they emerged into the vehicle bay, occasionally used by the telecom company for their fleet of vehicles. Now though, it was empty aside from a small crowd milling around a large entryway. As Mohammed and Rachel approached, they could see a group of people on the ramp leading to the surface.

"What's going on?"

A dust-covered woman turned to look at the pair. "Oh, hey Starsy, Mo'."

"Hey."

"How's it going, Iz'?"

"Not good. They've been trying to get the hatch open for about twenty minutes now. Starting to feel a bit claustrophobic down here."

Rachel nodded towards the group of burly people, grunting, heaving and counting loudly prior to more failed shoving attempts. "No-one tried cutting it open?"

"Oh. We… They don't think it's locked. Something from the building above has fallen onto it."

"And of course, it opens outwards…"

Izzy nodded. "The way the ramp's designed-"

"I get it… Just a pain in the arse is all. Really didn't plan on spending my weekend here."

Izzy grinned. "You and me both. Got me out of a wedding at least."

Mohammed smiled. "My congratulations to the happy couple."

"We'll see how happy they are once we get out of here." Izzy nodded. "But thanks, Mo."

"So what?" Rachel asked. "We just hang around here until they get that door open? Isn't there another way out?"

"If there is, we haven't found it."

Rachel rocked back on her heels, then leaned against the doorframe. "This is bollocks."

Izzy nodded, pulling out the collar on her shirt. "All these people, getting kinda stuffy too. You wanna go exploring? Maybe we can find-"

She was cut short by panicked shouting. Through the cacophony, Rachel heard one voice clearly. "Watch out! It's going!"

Rachel grabbed Izzy and pulled her back while shouting to Mohammed. "Move it!"

Following her lead, he grabbed the person closest to him and pulled them clear of the incoming avalanche of screaming people and debris.

Rachel waved him on. "Keep going! Out of the way!"

Mohammed and his new companion took cover behind a rolling toolbox while Rachel and Izzy found a sturdy concrete column. They watched as people ran by.

"Move to the sides!" Rachel shouted. "Idiots. Why are they running in line with it?"

A brick bounced down the ramp and hit the ground a few feet away. The corner chipped off, sending a spray of stones and dust into her face.

"Bleugh!"

"Damn!" Izzy spat and coughed, then glanced to Rachel. She had a cut on her forehead. "Are you okay? You're bleeding."

"I'll live." She tugged the hood over her head and cautiously glanced back to the door. "Looks like it's stopped. Come on, people might need help."

Mohammed checked that his new friend was okay, then joined the girls as they searched through the rubble.

Rachel kicked a breeze block out of her path. "Jesus... looks like a whole building..." She glanced up to the hatch. "And that other side still hasn't come through. Okay... Hey, Mo!"

He glanced over. "What's up?"

"Can you do me a favour, keep everyone back? It still isn't safe."

"Hey, Starsy! Got someone over here!"

Rachel clumsily jumped over a pile of bricks and onto a radiator before charging towards Izzy. "Where- Oh."

Barely visible under a layer of grey dust, a pair of bloodshot eyes and bright white teeth stared back at her.

"Here… Help me move this."

Rachel looked over and saw Izzy trying to lift a bent metal beam across his legs. She took the other end and on the count of three, managed to push it free. "Incoming!" Mohammed stepped clear as it came to rest at the bottom of the ramp. Once the dust settled, he gave her a thumbs up. "All good!"

"Can you walk?"

"I-" The man coughed and spat a dusty phlegm-ball on the floor. "I can barely… breathe."

"Mo, I need some heavy lifters up here!"

Taking his role as cordon guard seriously, Mohammed stopped each willing volunteer, briefly checked them for obvious wounds, then gave them the go ahead. Two large men were the first to arrive at Izzy's side, she pointed them towards the dusty mess on the floor.

As they set to work, Rachel raised a hand. "Wait, wait… sssh…"

Izzy bit her lip and tried listening. Sure enough, there was a light tapping, too rhythmic to be a natural sound. She and

Rachel both started walking cautiously through the rubble, and both came to a stop at the same place. They scurried to pull bricks off a PVC window frame, and carefully put it to one side. From under the detritus, a skinny teenager crawled forward, his face and hands covered in blood. Izzy froze as she laid eyes on him. "Are- Jesus wept, are you alright?"

"Yeah…" He replied, dazed. Rachel helped him to his feet, then continued to hold on when he took a tumble forward. "What happened?"

"As much as I'd love to discuss this…" Rachel nodded down the ramp. "There might be others. And he obviously needs medical attention."

As they cautiously made their way to the bottom, the 'heavy lifters' had found somewhere for their patient and were heading back up. "What can we do?"

"Look for people." She tilted her head toward the hatch. "And be careful of that thing."

"Got it."

Ahead of them, Mohammed was pointing at something beyond the main door. "Bring him over here! We've set up some beds!"

"Good thinking," Rachel replied as they hobbled closer.

Mohammed helped her carry him to a military cot, a holdover from the bunkers cold war days and laid him down.

She smiled at him as one of the 'volunteer nurses' approached. "You're in good hands now, just try and relax."

"Yeah… thanks… I uh… Didn't… name?"

"Oh. Sure. I'm Rachel, that's Izzy, and he's Mo'."

He raised his hand as if gesturing a sentence he wasn't saying. "Rake… I… uhh..."

"Easy now. We'll come chat once you're feeling a bit better."

"That… be nice…"

Rachel turned to leave but was accosted by one of the nurses. She tensed slightly as a damp cloth was pressed to her forehead.

"What-"

"Just a second. Better to clean it up now than risk an infection."

"Oh… I forgot about that."

The nurse dipped into an open Cold War era first aid box and dug out a sliver of tape and a gauze. "You'll have to forgive me, we're a bit low on modern equipment. It's sterile at least."

They passed the others on their way back towards the ramp. They were standing around, pointing up.

"What's going on?"

"We think it's about to go again. We couldn't find anyone else." Rachel briefly scanned the ramp, most of the large piles had been broken down and given at least a cursory glance by the rescuers. Eventually, her eyes settled at the creaking hatch side still in place. A trickle of water ran through the opening "I reckon it's gonna go any minute now. Tell everyone to get back into the bunker and wait until it's safe again."

The lifters dispersed to herd the rest back inside. Rachel watched them for a few seconds, then turned her attention back to the hatch.

"I hope I've still got a home to go back to." Izzy kicked a brick up the ramp and watched it roll back down.

"That was an old building." Rachel tried to sound reassuring. "Modern homes are built better than that. In reality, it was what? An earthquake and a bit more rain than we're used to. That shitty entrance hut will be an exception, not the rule."

Izzy frowned at her. "Who are you trying to convince?"

Mohammed raised his hands. "We won't know until we get up there and see it for ourselves."

Rachel nodded. "And we can't go until that other side comes in."

"We could give it some encouragement? I don't know about you, but I'm starting to get really sick of this hole."

"What are you suggesting?"

"I dunno? Throw some bricks? Hit it with a stick? I'm not spending another day down here just waiting for it to collapse."

"Only one of us should go. You and Mo' take cover."

"Why?"

Mohammed raised his hands. "I'm not going up there. Look at me, I've got the chiseled body of a computer technician, not an athlete."

Rachel laughed, then nodded to Izzy. "If you wanna do it, I don't mind. Just hope your running legs are up to it."

"I mean why do we have to split up? Between us, we could get it open, and protect one another."

Mohammed leaned down and prodded at the bent, dented panel that had been the right side of the hatch. "This thing looks kinda heavy, but you could use it for protection?"

Rachel shook her head. "Just something to get crushed under. Pile of bricks lands on that, you'll be scraping us up, not pulling us free."

"Oh."

"Come on," Izzy said, ascending the ramp. "The sooner we deal with this the sooner we can get out of here." She scooped up a chunk of rock on the way, and when she thought she was close enough, gave it a throw. It hit the ramp and bounced into the hatch, Rachel held her breath, but nothing happened.

"Damnit."

"Good shot though! Here, lemme try."

Another successful hit, but still no sign of movement.

"Damn. It's wedged in tight." Rachel moved farther up. "And we can't go up the open side because of all the rubble in the way." She picked up a chunk of brick and gave it another try.

The chunk bounced off the hatch, onto the ramp, then back into the hatch again. She heard a loud creaking, then a bang as the remaining hinge snapped. The hatch slammed into the ground, bringing with it another wave of trash and aged building materials.

"Move it!" She pushed away from the wall, jumped over

several breeze blocks, and fell into a run. Mohammed grabbed her as she reached the door. Izzy stumbled but scurried to one side on all fours as the first bricks, breeze blocks and chunks of rebar skidded to the bottom.

They covered their ears as a monstrous grinding reverberated around the garage, accompanied by loud bangs and pinging shards of bricks. Rachel kept her head low, her back turned, and could feel bits bouncing off her hoodie. The new avalanche had pulled with it a cloud of dust, a sickly yellow colour. Rachel could hear Izzy coughing, almost choking, but daren't look up.

She felt Mohammed turning, then heard him say something. She opened her eyes and saw that the debris had settled, flecks of dust danced in a beam of sunlight coming from the opening.

"Holy shit." She grinned and stood to full height. "We did it!"

Izzy retched spat and tried getting to her feet.

"So much for protecting each other." Rachel said as she helped her up. "Sorry, Iz'."

"Wa-" She spat again. "Wa'der."

"Oh! Er... Med bay! They'll have something!" She propped Izzy up and helped her to the makeshift hospital. Izzy pointed towards the table beside Rake. As she 'borrowed' from his bottle, a door in the distance creaked open.

"Is it safe?"

"No. Rachel replied, her shoulders drooping. "Just less dangerous. There's an opening, but be bloody careful!"

Mohammed shook his head. "Someone might hurt themselves."

"If they can get over the rubble, they're smart enough to get through that gap. Besides, most of the building is down here now." She motioned to the wreckage. "Probably nothing left to fall."

"Still, shouldn't we send a scout through first?"

Rachel shook her head. "Look at 'em, Mo'. They're already tired, agitated, it was a miracle they listened to us when they did." She shook her head. "No, let 'em do what they want. Besides, the more people go through, the less shit gonna be in our way when making our exit. Hopefully."

Izzy put the bottle back down and nodded her thanks to Rake. "That was a mess." She said, rejoining the others. "Gonna be coughing up dust for weeks."

"You, and about everyone else in this bunker." She motioned to the ramp, a somewhat orderly queue had formed. "At least they're going quickly. Shouldn't be waiting too long."

"Is it wrong that I expected cheering?"

Rachel shook her head. "Nah. But I guess they're too tired. I bet you're overwhelmed when you step out into fresh air again after all this time."

"Now that the door's open again… I dunno… feels like it wasn't really that long." She smiled, her teeth standing out from a dust-covered face. "And, I made some new friends, so hasn't been all bad."

As they stood around chatting, a murmur ran through the queue. It quickly turned to a shout, some started crying, others looked shocked.

"What's all this?" Rachel asked as she watched people coming back down.

Izzy shrugged. "No clue. Think we should go check it out?"

"Suppose it was too optimistic to think we'd solved all the problems today." She nodded. "Come on then."

A couple of people pushed by them, Rachel grabbed the third on the shoulders and asked, "What's going on?"

Looking up with a face covered in tears, she barely whispered. "Bodies, everywhere… Birmingham it's… destroyed."

"What?" Izzy glanced up the ramp.

"What do you mean Birmingham is destroyed? And bodies? What are you…"

"Let her go, Stars'…"

Rachel released her grip and watched the woman disappear out of view. "I need to see this. Ain't no way that little weather hiccup destroyed a city. Besides, how are you supposed to tell that from the entrance? Come on, something ain't right here."

Reaching the top of the ramp, Rachel let the last person out before following after. She crawled through the gap on her elbows, careful to avoid the rebar jutting out. Emerging onto the street, Rachel was blinded by the morning sun, but felt enormous relief as she filled her lungs with mostly fresh air. As her eyes adjusted, Izzy crawled out behind her, followed by Mohammed. Besides the people milling about, quietly talking to one another, the city was almost silent.

"This is…" Rachel looked up. Where there had once been tall

buildings, the sky now showed. She followed the skeletal metal structure back to street level, where torn up roads were blocked with overturned cars and the remnants of an office. Finally, her gaze settled on a shapeless mass by the crumbling wall protecting Anchor's entrance.

"This…" Izzy stepped forward. "This can't be…"

"How did this happen?" Rachel replied. "I thought- It was a little earthquake, and a bit of a storm. How did this happen?"

Mohammed shook his head, seemingly in disbelief. "It must have been worse than we thought."

"What the hell are we supposed to do now?" Izzy was clutching at her hair. "If these modern buildings… an entire city… my house… Jesus… And what happened to everybody else?"

"I know it looks bad, Iz', but reacting like this... I need you to- Izzy?"

"What are we supposed to do? Is it going to happen again? Are we the only survivors? What about these people?"

"Look." Rachel raised a finger. "Firstly, it ain't our job to look after this lot. Secondly, we've got a bunker we can use until we figure out our next move. We're obviously not going anywhere until these roads are clear, and I'd wager that while it looks bad here, we won't be the only survivors. Our families might have made it to safety. And damn it, Iz', until we see for ourselves, we don't know what's happened to our homes. So please, pull it together? I need you thinking if we're gonna get through this."

"Get through this?"

"You're being irrational! Yes, it's bad. But we survived! We're still breathing, and we might be able to fix this! But I can't do it alone!"

"Fix this? I-" Izzy paused, took a deep breath, and wiped the moisture from her eyes. "What do we do?"

"I don't know. But I know I can't do it on my ones." She surveyed the area again briefly, then turned back to Izzy and Mohammed. "The bunker is safe, but we need to get that hatch back in place in case it happens again. Also, there isn't enough food down there to support us, let alone everyone else."

"Uh…" Izzy wiped her face with her sleeves and inhaled. "Perhaps use hunger to convince others to help us?"

"Good thinking." She rubbed her chin. "Where's the nearest supermarket?"

Mohammed pointed down the street. "Go down this road, turn

right onto Newhall Street, left onto Lionel, follow it down until you reach the arched bridge thing. There's a row of shops there built into it, Quick-stop, and a continental food shop. Litu… Lithoo… Pah… L-something. should be food there. Maybe the bridge protected them too."

Izzy raised her hands. "If we go, we need to be careful not to look like looters."

Rachel nodded. "Another good point." She glanced to the other survivors milling about. "You seem to know the city pretty well, Mo'. Mind going on a little excursion?"

"On my own?"

"No. Try finding some volunteers. Let them know you're going for food. Bring back as much as you can. Food and water. And, if you find anyone else, let them know about this place. It's probably safer than anything they've got."

Mohammed nodded. "Consider it done." He turned and called out to the dazed survivors. A small group eventually formed near him to listen. Some nodded their heads in agreement, others were still overwhelmed by the situation. Eventually, he convinced six of them to join him, and they set off, climbing over the rubble and through the remains of buildings until they were out of sight.

"So what are we doing?" Izzy asked.

"We need to clear that ramp and get those hatches bent back into place."

"You think we're gonna see another storm?"

"I think I'd rather have the protection when it's time to find out."

Izzy nodded. "Yeah… yeah, fair point."

As they set to work clearing the entrance, the others saw what they were doing and came to help.

Despite the many hands, it still took over an hour to clear away the rubble. They had pushed it far from the opening, with the intention of avoiding a repeat lock-in experience.

"Right." Rachel said. "We should take a break, then get on with the ramp." She brushed herself off and stood back to admire their handiwork. They now had a clear path in and out of the bunker, and the largest chunks had been pushed as far from the opening as possible.

Izzy navigated through the people descending back into the

bunker and sat down on a tyre besides Rachel. "How do you think Mo's getting on?"

"Dunno. Sounded like a Satnav when we asked him about supermarkets though, so if anyone's gonna make it, he will."

"Why didn't you wanna go?"

"I... don't think I'm ready to see the city yet."

Izzy nodded. "Yeah... me either."

"Though..." She motioned to the hatch. "When we get that back in place, the ramp clear... we'll have to turn our attention to the streets."

"Oh? Sounds like you've been doing some thinking."

"Yeah. Had a lot of time to do that recently." She thumb-pointed down the road. "The 'closest' supermarket sounded like it was miles away. And what happens when we pick all the nearby places clean?"

Izzy looked to her with confusion. "The army or foreign aid will find us by then." She blinked. "Won't they?"

"I hope so. But we need to be prepared in case they don't. And what if that storm carried off all the local food?"

"What's your point?"

"We need a vehicle. Something powerful to clear the roads. Something able to tow cars." Rachel motioned to the hatch again. "But something that'll fit down here. Just in case."

"I don't know if your plan's crazy, or if I'm still trying to wrap my head around all this. Just look around, Starsy, modern buildings have fallen down around our ears and you're talking about finding a working truck? I don't think that makes sense."

"We need to do something."

"I don't know about you, but I haven't got the energy."

"Yeah…" Rachel could feel her belly rumble. "Hope Mo' gets back soon. I'm pretty hungry."

"Getting chilly out here too."

"Let's just go back inside for now. Have a look at those hatches."

As they descended the ramp, someone jumped the rubble and ran down to meet them.

"Hey, you Rachel?"

She nodded. "Yeah. You went with Mo' earlier, right?" She glanced at the radio in his hands. "We needed food. What's this?"

"It's coming. But Mo' thought you should hear this." He clicked the radio on and turned it up, pointing the aerial back out the hatch.

Izzy squinted. "It's really faint."

"Sssh, let me listen."

"*...is Private Edwards requesting any military personnel and reserves in or near Norfolk to make their way to the following coordinates...*"

3. Gathering - Ross Niles

Major General Ross Niles looked out over the flood of
confused faces with a stern frown. Less than sixty trained
military personnel stood before him, and they all knew about
as much as he did. For a brief second, he wondered if the lack
of numbers would benefit them in the long run. He was quick
to shut those thoughts down, replacing them with a silent
prayer of hope for whatever remained of his army. He counted
again. Fifty-five. Inhaling the damp stale air, he stepped
forward, hoping to still have the same number of people
standing before him at the end.

"Your attention."
The crowd turned as one to face him. An odd mix of dull
civilian clothing, modern army equipment, and bright hi-viz
jackets. Niles cleared his throat and looked around.
"Firstly, I'm glad you survived and were able to make your way
here." He raised his hands to the dark grey walls illuminated
by the floodlights either side of him. "As of this moment, King's
Lynn Civil Defense Bunker is your new home."
He waited for the unsure glances and thinned eyes to pass

before continuing.

"Two days ago, the United Kingdom experienced a sudden cataclysmic weather event. From the primary reports some of you have given me, and from what I've seen with my own eyes, we're living through an unprecedented disaster." He spoke slowly and calmly, allowing his words time to sink in. "I've heard nothing from the government. Nor have I heard anything from neighbouring countries or our allies. As far as I am aware, there are no plans to facilitate foreign aid or rescue, nor anyone currently available to offer such assistance." He took a deep breath. "We are on our own."

Niles allowed them a few seconds of discussion before clearing his throat again. The room fell silent in an instant. "Which brings me onto my next point. Anyone who wishes to walk out that door is welcome to do so. You have no obligation to stay here other than your willingness to help your brothers and sisters through this difficult time. Before you make your decision, however, consider that we have security here, food for some time, clean drinking water, a radio, and I will make it a priority task to search for loved ones and other survivors. We are also in close proximity to several other bunkers.

Bunkers that are full of civilians that need people like us to help them. All of us."

From the front row, a familiar face stoically smiled at Niles. His shoulders noticeably relaxed just slightly, and he waved the woman up to his side. As she approached, he shook her hand and leaned in. "Reyes. It is a relief to see you."

"Mutual, sir." She nodded to the crowd. "I'm staying. Back to speech."

Niles grinned as Tina Reyes stepped off to the side. With a trusted friend at his side, Niles straightened up and addressed the room with confidence.

"What I'm asking isn't easy. We don't even know where to begin, and all I can offer are the very basics in exchange for what will be exhausting and demanding work. But it might be our only chance at surviving. It might be the only chance this country has left." He raised a hand to the door. "Will you take that chance?"

* * *

Reyes closed the door behind her as Niles slumped into a

museum piece wooden chair with dusty red cushions. He let out a sigh as the dust settled.

"Not your best address, sir."

"Six." He said, his eyes drifting across the room in a daydream. "Forty-nine…"

"If I may…"

His attention snapped to Reyes. He gave an unsure nod.

"The losses mean food will last longer. I believe we need time, not manpower, sir."

He waved a hand. "Speak freely, Reyes, we're friends."

She let out a sigh, her entire body slumped slightly as she exhaled. "If help isn't coming, then our focus should be on long-term survival. We need to be entirely self-sufficient, fewer mouths to feed gives us the time to focus on that."

"We also have a responsibility to the other survivors," Niles replied in a matter-of-fact tone. "Priority one should be ensuring our own survival, of course." Niles weaved his fingers, the chair creaked under him as he relaxed back further. "But if we're talking about the long term, then we can't alienate those people. We may need to recruit them one day, or live with them if their bunkers fail."

Reyes studied him for a few seconds as if deciding whether to speak or not. "If we're talking the long run, have you considered your own position? How long can you lead these people? What happens when they start calling for votes? Or worse, accuse you of being a dictator?"

Niles' eyes thinned, his face turned red. "This is obviously a crisis situation. There might not be an army anymore, but there's still a chain of command. I did my duty, I have the experience, I've led these people before, and I will continue to lead them until this crisis is over."

"And how do you plan on accomplishing that?"

Niles drew breath to reply, then paused. He stood up and crossed the room to a glass panel. He picked off the plastic triangles and wiped the dust away before reaching for a marker.

"We have a total of forty-nine men and women at our disposal."

"Last check, twelve working vehicles, including a Cromwell."

Niles stopped scribbling. "We've got a tank?"

"Lefty and Dans brought it in. It's how they survived."

"And who gave those two a working tank?"

"It was advertising for a paintball site."

"Are there many functioning tanks left in the U.K. that I should know about?"

Reyes' face contorted into thought, then, she nodded. "The Tank Museum probably didn't survive, but the vehicles likely did. They have… er, had, quite the collection."

Niles frowned, his attention returning to the board. "That collection could outfit an army. We'll need to keep it in mind." He tapped the pen against his chin. "Wouldn't want it falling into the wrong hands."

"Noted."

"So… Forty-nine. Let's go with four teams of ten, one of nine. I want the specialists divided as evenly as possible. And if we can manage it, at least one mechanic in each team."

"I can assign Lefty, and…" Reyes looked to the ceiling. "I think Hadrian are both mechs. We'd do better with a list of personnel." She glanced behind her. "And an assistant to go get such things."

"For now, we'll manage. Give them a few more minutes to settle in."

He scribbled the headings 'Food, Water, Medicine' and 'Days' onto the board and stepped back.

"Is that 'days' since it happened?"

Niles nodded. "Two and a half so far… My earliest report

suggests it first struck on Saturday morning. If I can still trust my watch, it's Monday afternoon." He looked back at Reyes as she wrote in a water-damaged notepad. "I don't think I asked, how did you survive?"

"I got lucky." She replied flatly. "I was walking the dogs when it happened. Took shelter in a pillbox till it passed. It didn't pass, so using my trusty trench shovel I-"

"You just carry a shovel around with you?"

"It's for burying the dog poo. It's collapsable."

Niles rolled his eyes. "Go on."

"I literally dug in for the weekend. Covered the doorway, got a fire going, rationed out some sausage roll between me and the dogs. Thought it was kinda funny actually. I walk by that thing every time I have to take them out, always thought it would never get used again, then I'm the one who has to use it." She frowned. "Well, it was funny, until I saw the aftermath."

"It's a good thing we never demolished these places."

"Indeed." She looked down at her pad, then back up at Niles. "How did you survive?"

"Some of the younger lads needed a respectable tour guide and by happy coincidence, I was due to visit this place anyway to see if it could be made useful again or should be destroyed to make way for newer facilities. Like you, the weather forced us to stay. Sent out a scout this morning, they returned with bad news. Been here ever since trying to contact survivors on the radio."

"I heard the broadcast. It's what brought me here."

"A few civilians too…" Niles replied, his expression dropped. "We sent them to other bunkers, gave them advice on how to survive. Some were angry. Others were thankful… probably just being polite."

Reyes shook her head. "We've only got limited supplies."

"Oh, it's more than just that. This bunker is our base of operations for the foreseeable future. There will be plenty of survivors out there looking for a place like this to call their own. We need to be on high alert, but we also need to be open to the idea that some civilians could be useful to us. After we establish ourselves here properly, we should look into the viability of recruiting them, training them up. Until then, this place is all we've got."

Reyes sighed. "I can understand why you'd want to help them… uh, use them to help us... but really our priority should be the here and now. How should we proceed?"

"We need that list of personnel. I think they've had enough

time to find a space by now so let's sort that out."

"I'll get it done," Reyes said, rising to her feet. "Will, that be all?"

"For now."

As the door closed again, Niles filled in the last of the details, then sat back down. He stared through the board, daydreaming until a knock roused him from his thoughts.

"Come in." He replied, absentmindedly.

It was one of the soldiers who'd made it to the bunker wearing kit assembled from civilian stock. World War 2 style webbing with a hole in the left shoulder sat over a hooded camouflage coat.

"Major General."

"At ease."

If he had relaxed, Niles hadn't seen it.

"You have something to report?"

"Two things, sir."

"Go ahead."

"My assessment is that this group is under-equipped for the situation, I believe I can rectify this."

Niles rested his elbows on the arms of the chair and weaved

his fingers in front of his face. "Oh?"

"RAF Marham is almost directly south of here. I believe we can use the equipment stored there to outfit the soldiers here."

Niles thought for a moment, then nodded slowly. "Perhaps other survivors there as well."

"Yes, sir."

"I will keep it in mind." The chair creaked as he relaxed back. "The second thing?"

"A personal request."

"Go on."

"I grew up a stone's throw away from this bunker. I know the area well. With this in mind, I'd like to offer my knowledge should it be required."

"Thank you for informing me…"

"Corporal Henk, sir."

Niles made a mental note, then nodded. "Thank you, Corporal."

With nothing more than a salute, Henk turned on the spot and headed through the door.

Niles was studying the board when Reyes returned. She'd found a clipboard, although it looked too small for the pile of papers sitting on top.

"Good news." She said, putting the pile down on a dust-covered filing cabinet. "We had three more turns up, they agreed to stay."

"That is good news…" Niles replied quietly.

"I've got some bad too, I'm afraid." Reyes rubbed the bridge of her nose as if trying to dislodge a smell. "The main toilets for the bunker are nonfunctional. I've closed them off and directed people to the functioning loos, but the mains will need cleaning and connecting if we want to use them."

"More problems to deal with. Add it to the list." He turned away from the board and looked at Reyes. She wore a smile, despite looking extremely tired. His gaze drifted to the pile. "I assume these are our personnel files?"

"Yes."

"A far cry from the computer system…" He replied, crossing the small room. He picked up the clipboard and thumbed through it.

"Fifty-two now, you say?"

"Yes, sir. And it seems a good mix. Medics, engineers, although we might struggle to find a use for air assault."

Niles grinned, taking out one of the sheets. "Let's put the

teams together."

Reyes glanced around the room. "I don't suppose there's a desk hidden under all this dust?"

"Unfortunately not." He placed Henk's profile on the floor, then thumbed through for another.

"Corporal Henk, sir?"

Niles nodded. "Know his type. Useful, but I need to keep an eye on him."

"Oh?"

"A gut feeling. For now, he's in Bravo Team. Ah…" He sighed. "These two…"

"I assume you mean Lefty and Dans?" Reyes blew the air out of her cheeks. "If you split them up, they might just leave."

"And if they leave, they might become a bigger problem in the future." Niles placed the pair down beside Henk. "Charlie Team. Need someone reliable, someone trustworthy to lead them. A good influence."

"Major Luke Warwick, sir?"

Niles nodded his approval. "Didn't he make LC?"

"I believe he was due for promotion prior to the weather anomaly."

"We'll have to see how much the old system still means over

the next few weeks." Niles sighed, placing Luke Warwick's sheet down above Lefty and Dans. "I have a feeling we're going to be making a lot more changes in the future." "Re-organizing in this way is unprecedented, but then I suppose we've never dealt with anything like this before."

It took over an hour to organize and reorganize the piles into five different teams, named Alpha, Bravo, Charlie, Delta, and Echo. Reyes would lead Alpha, while the others were to be handled by their own team leaders.

Reyes sat on the floor, her back against the filing cabinet, her eyes red with tiredness. "Some people won't be happy with being passed over for leadership."

"There isn't much I can do about that." He picked up the pile for Charlie team. "And if they're the professionals I think they are, their focus should be on bigger problems."

Reyes didn't reply, Niles could sense the limits of her patience had been reached and decided against further discussion. Instead, he checked his watch then looked at her. "We should eat, sleep, then in the morning, we'll share the plan with them."

Reyes nodded slowly then climbed to her feet. She stretched

out, her spine cracking with a noise that even Niles felt relief from, "See you in the morning then. What time?"

"Early. O'five-hun-"

A knock at the door startled them both. Reyes stepped clear as Niles reached for the handle. Opening the door revealed a young woman wearing full battle-dress. She was breathing heavily but stood to attention when she saw the Major General.

"Sir. Lieutenant Yasmir."

Niles' eyes thinned. "Something the matter?"

"Two more soldiers have turned up. They came from Kelvedon Hatch, reporting that a sizable civilian population exists there. Currently, they have food and water, but no working radio."

"We've got several bunkers nearby that need our help, why is… 'Kelvedon Hatch' any different?"

"They've got people venturing out, salvaging. Corporal Henk thinks we would benefit from contact with such a group, for area information, and to trade their salvaged goods with our own supplies for variety. It is his belief that we should provide them with a radio."

Niles frowned. "So why are you here, and not the Corporal?"

"He asked me to relay the information, sir."

The frown didn't fade. "Very well. I shall consider this. But, Lieutenant, I expect Corporal Henk to deliver his own messages in the future. Make this clear to him, thank you."

"Of course, sir." She offered a sharp salute, then turned and disappeared down the corridor.

"I see what you mean…" Reyes replied as she stepped through the door. "I'll keep an eye on him too."

"He's only part of the problem. People who think they know best despite minimal experience…"

Reyes raised a hand. "People with experience can be stubborn. Set in their ways. You're going to need fresh perspectives if we're going to get through this."

Niles sighed. "I can already see challenges on the horizon-"

"So, use it." She was getting visibly annoyed now. "You're going to need all the help you can get, and, if I know you, any challenges will be turned to your advantage, used to strengthen your position instead of weakening it."

Niles drew breath to reply but was cut short.

"And this is about more than the army now. This is about survival. Things have changed."

"I know, Tina, believe me, I know."

"Knowing and understanding are different things."

Before he could reply, Tina nodded sharply and turned.

"See you tomorrow. Five sharp."

Niles watched her turn the corner to a cracked wall, then, when he was sure she was out of earshot, replied. "Yeah. Tomorrow."

4. Reality - Jack Mason

There was a crunch, then a gasp of relief.

A scaffolding tube fell away from the wheel brace and rolled down the road. A lone figure watched as it came to a stop against half a caravan, then turned his attention back to his problem; A flat tyre, caused by the remains of a jagged metal fence. A well-used toolbox by the spare wheel had 'Jack Mason' scratched into the lid. The letters shone a dull amber in the evening sun.

Standing up, and tucking the lugnuts in his top pocket, Jack reached into his van, fishing around for a cigarette. He paused for a moment and listened. He thought he could hear the music. After a few seconds, he popped open the door and climbed inside. Sitting in the driver's seat, Jack glanced over the dash and saw the radio glowing a faint green.

"Eh. Found one, did you? One-oh-eight FM? Hmm?"

He turned the volume dial and glanced under the curtain separating the cab from the back of his van. A stain covered mattress, a few cardboard boxes full of food, a gas stove, and a pile of salvaged tools, all where he'd left them when the tyre had blown. He pulled the curtain down again, and relaxed as much as he could on the grotty, torn seat.

A soft, grandfatherly voice filled the van. *"-Sinatra, with Blue Moon. In a few minutes, we'll be moving into the seventies with some Queen, and Abba, but before then folks I think we should have a little chat."*

"There's a station out here?" Jack blew the air out of his cheeks, cranked the dial and went back to work.

"I'm no meteorologist…" The volume made the voice sound harsh, but Jack was just happy to have some background noise. *"…so I won't even try to speculate on what happened. But the results are obvious."*

"No shit," Jack mumbled as he wrestled with the spare.

"I've only been to the surface once since it happened. I still can't quite believe it."

"Yeah…" Jack sighed, glancing up the road to the scrapyard of cars littering the motorway. "You and me both, buddy."

"I don't know why I set this radio up but talking about it… I suppose it's a coping mechanism. Helps me figure out my thoughts. And we all need a little music in our lives, regardless of whether the world has ended."

Jack scrunched his face. "Is it the world though? Or just here?"

"But we all need to do more if we're going to survive. Does anyone know if it's going to happen again? Will it get worse? Are there places we can go? I wish I could tell you to call the hotline, but word of mouth will have to do. Tell people to listen to One-Oh-Eight FM, and I'll do my best to share the latest news. I've got a couple of survival manuals down here too, might make for some interesting bedtime reading."

"Eh. Good thinking." Jack tightened the last of the lugnuts down and jumped up.

"This is all assuming, of course, that I'm not alone, and there are other people out there who made it to shelter in time. If not then..."

"I'm here," Jack replied.

"Well... doesn't bare thinking about, does it? Incidentally, and I don't recommend this, but if you happen to be in the area, come to say hello. Maybe give me a lift too? Getting kinda stuffy down here, old records don't make for the best company." He read off a set of directions and coordinates. Jack mentally checked his map. "Sorry, buddy. I've got my own path. Good luck to ya though."

"I'll be here. Anyway, let's get back to the music. It's the Seventies at Seven, and to kickstart this party, Stevie Wonder, with Superstition."

Jack gathered his tools and tossed them in through the side door. He heard something in the distance, but couldn't see anything. Jumping in the van proper, he leaned through the curtain and turned the radio down.

His eyes thinned as the noises grew louder. A fierce engine grunting somewhere close by, the sound of metal grinding against metal. Then he saw it, rolling over cars and pushing trucks out the way as it stormed towards him.

"What...?"

It didn't show any signs of slowing down. Jack slammed his hand into the warning light button and scurried out the side door. He fell into a run towards the closest vehicle. Climbing on top of an overturned car, he peeled his shirt off from under his coveralls and waved it frantically. He couldn't be sure if they'd seen him or the lights.

Jack knew a Mercedes Unimog when he saw one. It towered

over him, a monster of a vehicle with a snapped log sticking out of the bumper. It fell off as the vehicle slowed, then pulled to a stop just short of him.

He was surprised when the door creaked opened, and a fresh-faced woman, no taller than five feet, jumped out and smiled at him.

"Hello!"

Jack tried to elegantly pull his shirt back on. "Uhh... Hi?"

"I'm Ada." She slammed the door shut and wandered over as he jumped off the car.

"Jack."

"Good to meet you, Jack."

"Likewise..."

She grinned. "Right, well now that we've got the awkward small talk out the way, you mind if I ask what you're doing out here?"

"Changing a tyre. What about you?"

"Looking for survivors."

Jack nodded. "Found one."

"So I see." She glanced around. "Just one?"

He eyed her suspiciously. "Yes?"

"Hmph." She folded her arms and sighed. "You're the second

living person I've found."

"How long you been out?"

"Since the Storm passed…" Her gaze drifted back to him and she fixed him with a stare. "So, what are you planning on doing tonight?"

He pointed down the way she'd come. "Was gonna keep pushing through this mess for another hour or so, then pull up and cook some dinner."

"But… since I just cleared that route for you, you've got some free time now, right?"

Jack glanced at the snapped log between them. "I suppose I do."

"And eating alone is pretty boring, right?"

"I suppose it is."

"Well, aren't you glad I came along when I did! How about, you start a fire, find a gas stove or something, and I see what I've got in the Moggy."

He watched as she climbed into the truck and dug around in the passenger area. After a few seconds, Jack wandered back to his van and searched through his equipment. After wistfully looking at the gas cooker, he instead opted to carry a small pile of wood back to the clearing. With a little persuasion to get it going, Jack was soon warming his fingers by a reasonably sized fire.

"Ah! A nice cozy campfire. You know how to treat a lady at the end of times."

"Oh. I wasn't-"

Ada grinned. "Relax, just teasing." She tossed a couple of cans over.

"What's this?" He asked, catching them both. "Sausage and beans?"

"Yeah. Sorry, I ran out of steak and caviar on Friday."

Jack smiled, ripped the labels off, and pulled out a knife. He carefully cut the lids open and placed them in the fire. "I've been on the ready to eats. The real budget ones. This practically is steak and caviar."

Ada watched the dancing flames with flickering interest. "Is that how you've survived?"

"Partly." Jack motioned back the way he'd traveled. "My grandad had an auxiliary hide on his property. Was staying with him when..." He motioned around. "...all this."

"What's that?" Ada asked, prodding at the fire with a stick.

"What's what?"

"Auxiliary hide…?"

"Oh. It's like a little shelter. For a small team."

"Wait, your grandad just had one of these handy?"

"It'd been there since the second world war. If the nazi's ever made it to British soil, I think the idea was to do some guerrilla fighting from the hides." He motioned to her. "What about you?"

"The back of this thing was open, parked between a bank and a pub. Most of the pub ended up on top. Bank was a good cover though."

"You just found it?"

Ada nodded. "Yep. Took cover in the Moggy. Was kinda hoping someone would turn up and drive me away from it all. My knight in shining armour never showed though, so I took matters into my own hands."

Jack gave the cans a slight shake with a Y-shaped twig, then relaxed back, half-listening to Ada.

"Found a spare key in the glovebox… Or I guess it was an old key? Kinda rough but it still works. Good thing too, I don't know the first thing about stealing a truck. When the weather died down a bit, I just rolled out of there, Moggy brushed off the pub like it was trash."

Jack glanced up at it. "Damn… what a beast."

"Like it was made for this." She pointed to the cans. "You wanna sort that out?"

"Oh! Yeah. Sure. You got a bowl or something?"

"A bowl? I've got a spoon and a thick glove." She laughed. "A bowl? Someone isn't getting into the spirit of this end of days scenario."

"You been listening to the radio?"

"There's a radio out here?"

He nodded. "One oh eight FM. The guy on there said he can't believe this happened. I guess I still can't either. Feels like I been in a trance since…"

"Really? This has been pretty liberating for me." She accepted the can offered by Jack's makeshift twig tongs, and set it down in front of her to cool. "Given me a chance to put my old life behind me. Forget all the inconsequential shit that I used to think about." Ada adopted an exaggerated voice. "Hey, Ada, remember that time at school you did that stupid thing? Yes brain, thanks for that. Or what about that other time when you did that? That was really embarrassing eh?" She shrugged. "Don't matter anymore. If anyone else survived who remembers that shit, well…" She motioned to the world around them. "More pressing matters I think."

"That's it?"

"No of course not. Just one way of looking at it. Alright, how about this. This Armageddon is a good thing, Earth's way of saying 'Nah, you fucked it up, get off.' The planet can heal now. You ever see those pictures of Chernobyl? Like how nature just took over again?"

"You mean the picture of the Ferris wheel?" Jack frowned. "If that's what's in store for England, then that's… that's really sad. I still can't imagine how many people have already been killed, and for the country to just fade away like that?"

"You can't change what's happened, Jack."

"No. I… suppose I can't."

"So you need to embrace it. Buildings might have fallen, but they're still full of treasures." She dug her fork out and picked up her can. "Besides, what did you do before this?"

"Mechanic."

"What, for like cars and vans and stuff?"

He nodded. "Yeah. Ran a garage in the States before coming back to visit."

"Oooh? America, huh?" She squinted. "You haven't got a yank

accent… There long?"

"Not long enough, apparently." He replied, motioning around again.

"Hmph. Well, regardless, my next point would be easier to make if you'd worked some shitty office job. Still though, imagine what you can do with your life now you've got the whole country to explore. No more customers to deal with, and the repairs you make out here actually mean something. You're not just trying to pass an M.O.T. anymore, this is the difference between life and death! Isn't that more exciting than checking people's headlights are properly aligned?"

"You're saying I should be thankful that failing to make a repair means I could die?"

Ada nodded. "It sounds dumb when you put it like that, but yeah." She waved her fork at the surrounding wrecks. "There's no-one around to give you a ticket anymore, no-one to enforce a bunch of arbitrary rules, no-one to stop you doing whatever the hell you want. You're never gonna have to fill in another form as long as you live. Never have to pay taxes again. We're getting back to real living! Where the work we do actually means something. We've all spent so long as part of the system, we've forgotten how to live without it."

"Oh." Jack frowned. "I get it. You're some sort of anarchist."

Ada laughed. "No. More like a realist. Bad shit has happened, but what are the benefits? Well, I never passed my driving test, yet I get to drive this weapon about, that's awesome!" She jammed a forkful of beans in her mouth, barely chewed, swallowed, and continued. "And if I find somewhere I like, I can just plot up there, build a house from the bits lying about, no planning permission, no paying for materials, no-nonsense."

Jack raised his hands. "But think about everything we've lost! How long do you think it'll take to repair airports for example? Or power plants? Soon all this fuel will go bad, we'll run out of food. If help doesn't come soon, we're finished."

"Wow, you're a real downer, you know that, Jack?"

"Maybe I'm the realist."

"Ha. Well, I suppose time will tell, won't it?"

Jack scooped up his can and dug in with his knife. "Yeah. I suppose it will."

They ate in silence. When they were finished, Jack picked a burning stick off the fire and lit a cigarette.

"You smoke?"

Ada shrugged. "Sure."

Jack passed one over before relaxing back. He pondered using the can as an ashtray, then glanced around, seemingly remembering where he was.

"Where you headed next?"

She shrugged again, taking a drag on her smoke. "Dunno. Was hoping to run into more people."

"Yeah. Me too."

"Maybe we're just the first ones to try driving about out here?"

"Yeah…" Jack nodded absentmindedly. "Maybe so."

"So what? You wanna stick together? We'd make a good team, Moggy and…"

"Just Transit, thanks."

"So what d'ya say? Partner?"

"I…" Jack studied her with narrow eyes. "I don't know anything about you. How do I know you won't just disappear in a pinch, or worse, steal my stuff?"

"I should be worried about you stealing my shit!" Ada replied, jabbing in his direction with the cigarette and a grin. "As far as I know, all you've got is a van full of firewood." She shook her head. "No, this is purely practical. You watch my back, I watch yours, and together we might just survive out here long enough to find some other people."

"How would we handle this? And how do I know you're not just gonna ignore my instructions?"

"Well, you don't." Ada gave him a toothy smile. "If they're dumb instructions, of course, I'll ignore them. But alright, Mr. U.S.A. we can set some ground rules."

Jack sighed. "Doesn't look like I've got much of a choice here."

Ada's expression soured. "Look, I'll be honest, we might survive out here individually, right? But actually, if we work together, that chance of survival increases. And believe me, I wanna survive. That won't happen if I turn grizzled mother-fuckers like you into enemies, so it's sorta in my best interests to stay on your good side."

"Grizzled mother-fu-" Jack shook his head. "You're not looking for a partner, you're looking for a bodyguard."

"I'm looking for both, and you look like a package deal."

"Jeez…" Jack glanced up at the Unimog, then back down at Ada. "Fine. We'll work together, but if this turns out to be a bad deal, I'm gone, alright? We both go our separate ways."

"Sounds good to me." Ada's smile returned. "Moggy's good at pushing stuff out the way, and you can keep it running, right?"

He sighed. "Parts are gonna be hard to find."

"Won't need parts, ain't nothing out here stronger than this."

Jack blew a cloud of smoke skyward. "We'll see."

"So, partner, what's the plan?"

"I'm headed to London. Probably loads of people there."

"Looking for someone in particular?"

"Hoping my family survived. Had an estate in the countryside."

"Oh, fancy."

"After seeing all this, it'll be a miracle if it's still standing."

"I hope they made it, your family I mean."

"If anyone did, it'd be them. Stubborn folk, you know?"

"I can imagine."

Jack flicked his cigarette over the barrier and got to his feet.

"Hopefully get to them quickly with your help."

"I'll do what I can." Ada yawned and stubbed her smoke out underfoot. "Been a hard day. Think I'm gonna get some sleep."

Jack nodded. "Alright. Thanks for the food."

"No problem, glad to have someone to share it with. Good night, Jack."

Ada gave him a wave as she climbed up the side-steps into the rear cabin. The setting sun reflected off the windscreen, and for a few minutes, Jack enjoyed the snapshot of serenity among the chaos.

A gentle breeze rolled through, just chilly enough to make him shiver. He zipped up his coveralls, stamped the fire out, and retreated to his van.

5. Another - Isabelle Jackson

At the entrance to Anchor, Izzy was sitting on a pile of tyres while her companion wandered back and forth.

"D'ya think she's alright?"

Izzy shrugged. "Dunno. Hope so."

"Think she's gonna find something?"

"I don't know, Rake." Izzy turned away and sighed with irritation. "Just wait and see."

She glanced over to the remains of the entrance, a gap in an otherwise destroyed wall. Beyond it, the roads leading away from the bunker had been cleared. Anything worth salvaging had long since been pulled into Anchor, while the less useful, broken, or trash items had been pushed farther out. Izzy watched a couple of people walking through the twisted metal frame of what was once an office building, picking through the rubble for anything they deemed useful. Under one of the stairways, a couple of skinny teenagers were trying to get a vending machine back on its feet.

"You think we should go look for her?"

Izzy sighed again. "No."

"She could be in trouble though."

"Starsy? I don't think so. She was practically made for this world."

"Still though-"

"Raaaaaake," Izzy replied, waving her arms. "Just relax. If we went looking, we'd be the ones need rescuing. She'll be back when-" She raised a finger as the tell-tale rumble of an engine in the distance caught her attention. "See, told you."

"Hope she brings back something big! Just imagine it! The two of us, out here, clearing roads, salvaging whatever we want!"

Izzy tried to hide a shudder. "Uh... Have you thought about getting your own vehicle?"

"What? Why?"

"Er, well, I'd like my own space. And if you had your own van, you'd be able to carry more stuff, go where-ever you wanted."

"Oh. I don't wanna go anywhere." He blinked. "Wait, weren't you just gonna hang around at Anchor and salvage locally? Duck back into the bunker when you had the stuff to bring in?"

"I'm not staying here, Rake. This place is a death-trap."

"Anchor saved us all though, how can you say that?"

"It won't last. This bunker is properly ancient, full of asbestos, there's no food, the water pumps barely work, and the ventilation shaft is blocked." She ran a hand through her dusty, frizzy hair. "It's too much work to repair. We should be trying to find somewhere else. Hack Green... or Lawford Heath, they were modernized. Would have survived all this much better, would be fully stocked."

"How come you know so much about these places? I thought they were supposed to be secret?"

"Some of them were... Most of them were decommissioned though, sold to private entities." Izzy glanced back to the entrance. "Before all this happened, I used to run an Urbex blog. That's how I know about these places. Was getting a tour of the new garage facilities here when the disaster struck."

Rake looked at her with a blank stare.

"Ugh. Urbex? Urban exploration?"

He shrugged.

"I used to go into old, abandoned, or derelict buildings, take photos, document the history, then I'd post about my adventures on the internet."

"Oh. I miss the internet."

Izzy rolled her eyes. "That bump on your head needs looking

at again, Rake."

"Oh. I'm fine!"

"Yeah. Sure."

"So… err... you know about bunkers?"

"Are you genuinely interested, or just trying to make small talk?"

"I wanna know!"

Izzy relaxed back against the tyres. "I've been to hundreds of interesting places, some multiple times. You get the tourist ones that everyone knows about, Kelvedon Hatch, Hack Green… They gave tours all the time. But if you wanted to find the hidden gems, you had to ask for permission, talk to people, organize groups, or hope that one of the companies would waste so much money adding a garage that they open it up for tours to recuperate some funds." She motioned to the entrance. "That's what happened here. The fleet garage ended up massively over budget, so they opened it up for tours." Izzy glanced back to Rake. "Speaking of which, how'd you end up here?"

"I was…"

"Yes?"

"Sorry… What was the question?"

She shook her head. "Nevermind."

Izzy was thankful when the growlings of the engine grew so loud they drowned out any further conversation Rake might have embarked upon. Hopping up to greet Rachel, Izzy was surprised to see an unfamiliar van approaching.

"Who's that?" Rake shouted over the noise.

"I don't know!" Izzy replied.

The large box van rolled to a stop, whoever was driving shut the engine off and rolled down the window. A jolly, but hollow-faced man with a huge grey beard and a grease-stained, loose-fitting cap smiled down at them.

"Hey, kids."

"Hi. I'm Rake!"

"Okay…" He blinked. "Uh. Good to meet you, Rake. I'm Stan, and this fine specimen is McTavish."

Another bearded man leaned over and nodded to the pair.

"Hoo's it Gaun?"

Rake grinned. "I'm good. You?"

"Nae baud." He pointed to Izzy. "An' why did they cry ye?"

Izzy shrugged. "Uh… Sorry?"

"She's Izzy." Rake said, grinning. "Saved my life."

"Glad to meet ye." He sat back and relaxed.

"Sounds like a good friend to have out here." Stan motioned to the entrance. "I take it this is Anchor? Met a girl out on the M40 said we could stay here?"

"You spoke to Rachel?" Izzy nearly jumped with excitement.

"Yes, this is Anchor, and yeah, you're welcome to stay here. Although I guess it isn't really up to me."

"Who's in charge?"

Izzy shrugged. "No-one really. I suppose Rachel? But she's off doing her own thing most of the time now."

"There's no-one leading you? How have you got so much done? The roads here are practically drivable compared to other places we've been."

"Dunno. Rachel sorta just starts doing something useful, and everyone else just copies her."

"I'll have to thank her next time I see her. So, Rake, Izzy, you think we can get this through that hole?"

Izzy stepped back and briefly, examined the box van. After scrunching her face for half a minute and glancing back to the hatch, she nodded. "Yes?"

"You don't sound so sure."

"Well… it's about the size of one of those cherry picker lorries, isn't it?"

"What's that got to do with anything?"

Izzy frowned. "I swear to god, I'm gonna write a leaflet for this place…" She exhaled and pointed to the entrance. "Anchor is an underground telephone exchange, with a garage, for telecoms vehicles. Ergo, if this van of yours fits the size of a common telecoms vehicle, it should go through that entrance. But! It's on you, okay? If you get jammed in the hole, you're the one driving, not me."

Stan glanced around, then nodded. "Go on then. Open it up."

Izzy nudged Rake on the shoulder and pointed him to the hatches. After a few seconds of heaving the mangled metal slabs out of place, Stan restarted the engine, lined up with the opening, and cautiously rolled forward.

Izzy watched with grit teeth as it rolled onto the soft incline, then onto the steeper drop into the garage proper. For the entire journey down, Izzy couldn't take her eyes off it, the tension was giving her a headache. Finally, and much to her relief, the box van rolled into the bunker without a problem. Rake waved back up to her and raised a thumb.

Izzy was midway through a sigh of relief when a honking horn made her jump.

"Ugh! Damnit." She turned to see Rachel's tow truck rounding the corner. She was still honking the horn when she pulled to a stop.

"Izzy! Izzilla… Izz-waaaaaan."

"Welcome back! You look like shit, Starsy."

"Yeah, but I feel like a million dollars." She jumped out and motioned for Izzy to follow her around the crumbling wall to the vehicle she'd been pulling. "Wait till you see-"

"A Land Rover?" Izzy nearly flattened Rachel with a hug. "Oh my god, you're the best!"

"Ooof. You're welcome."

When Izzy finally released her grip, Rachel brushed herself off and stepped to one side.

"Defender. In blue, with chequer plating. Has held up extremely well considering the weather we've had."

"Where'd you find it?" Izzy asked, peering through the still intact windows.

"Farmhouse off the M40. Well… hidden under the remains of one, anyway."

"Does it work?"

"Sure does. Here." Rachel fished some keys out of her pocket, checked them, then tossed them over.

"It's got keys?"

"Like it was just waiting to be found. Wasn't a struggle to get it clear either."

"It's like destiny." Izzy pulled the door open and made a sweeping glance of the interior. "It's actually kinda nice in here."

"Despite the fact it was on a farm, and it's older than Rake, I'd say so. Oh, yeah! I got you some other bits too that might help."

Izzy joined her at the boot and followed Rachel's urgings to open it. A myriad of odd electronics and batteries stared back at her.

"Okay? I recognize the kettle, and the car battery, but the-"

"Not a car battery. Leisure battery."

"Er?"

"Car battery needs to start the motor, but that's like… a short, powerful burst, right? Not really too good for powering long-term electronic stuff on. This leisure battery, dug out of a caravan before I pushed it off the M-forty, is made for that stuff. And this..." She picked up a lump of metal with wires hanging off it. "...is an inverter. Turns the twelve volts from that battery into 'house power', so you can use things like the kettle, fan heater. But you gotta be careful not to drain the battery. You need a split charge relay to charge it, or..." She shrugged. "I dunno, solar panels or something?"

Izzy blinked, then looked back to the boot full of wires and components. "The battery connects to the inverter, which lets me plug household stuff in."

"Yeah. Basically." Rachel closed the boot. "I tell you what, I found some tea bags and some milk that didn't smell. So I suggest we go inside, I show you how to set all this up, we do it, then we sit down and have a nice cup of tea."

"Oh my god, yes, Rachel. I could literally kill for a tea right now. That coffee Mo' brought back doesn't agree with me."

"Come on then, we've got work to do."

Izzy joined Rachel in the cab of her tow truck for the descent into Anchor. Rake waved when he saw them, but remained locked in conversation with McTavish and Stan.

"Ah yeah. I'd forgotten about those two." She switched the engine off and jumped out. With Izzy's help, she unhitched the

Defender and rolled it into the far corner. It bounced into a wrecked sofa someone had dragged in and rolled forward again before Izzy got to the handbrake.

"This looks awesome!" Rake said when he finally approached. Izzy and Rachel were digging through the wiring, untangling it and laying it on the floor neatly.

"You like?" Rachel replied with a grin.

"Oh yes. Very much."

Izzy motioned to the box van over the other side of the garage. "You making friends, Rake?"

His eyes lit up. "They want to trade!"

"Ah yeah," Rachel replied. "Food, medicine, that sort of thing. We should check it out once we're done here. Don't worry, I got a tidy haul myself today too."

After a lengthy poke around, Rake dropped onto the sofa and watched the girls work.

"Right." Rachel said, picking up the battery. "Where do you want this?"

"What do you mean?"

"Well... I suppose it doesn't need to be permanent, but we

should try not to waste any of this wire."

"I'm not sure I follow?"

"You've gotta think about the layout, right? You're gonna be traveling about in this, using it for a living. So you need to think about where you're putting the bed, the cooker, and all that stuff when you get it."

"Oh."

"You could do it a number of ways, but I think what's obvious is that the mattress will only go in lengthways, right?"

"Right."

"So you've got to make a decision, which side are you putting it on? And then from there, you can work out where all the free space is for the battery, inverter, all that stuff."

"I think I'll put the bed behind the passenger seat?"

"Could even take that out if you wanted. But yeah, sounds good."

"That means the battery would have to go on this side?"

"Yeah… And I suppose if you don't fix it down, you can always move it. I wouldn't recommend driving about with it like that though."

Izzy scrunched her nose. "So… what do we have to do?"

Rachel dragged the battery over and picked up a roll of wire.

"It's pretty self-explanatory. These wires connect to the battery, but we'll do that last so we're not throwing live cables about. So first thing, let's connect them to the inverter." She handed the wire over and pointed at the device. "I'll walk you through it, but if you don't know about this stuff, you should probably learn."

"Is this dangerous?"

"Ha. No. Not really. Well… no. Twelve volts is nice in that it doesn't kill you when it zaps you, just reminds you not to do that shit again. But since we're not hooked up to the battery yet, we're good."

"Uhh, I don't want to get zapped."

"It's fine. Just take it slow, and listen to me. It's all pretty self-explanatory anyway. Look." Rachel pointed to the dials on the back of the inverter. "Untwist those, put the red wire in the red slot, the black wire in the black slot, then screw the caps back on. Congratulations, you've just completed one half of the puzzle."

Izzy blinked, staring at the wires in her hand and the inverter. Carefully, she leaned down, and unscrewed the caps as instructed, fed the wires into the holes, then screwed it all back together.

"See?" Rachel said, grinning. "Easy peasy."

"But now, battery?"

"Relax. It'll be fine." She scooped up a couple of battery clips and held them out. "Right, now you're gonna need a screwdriver to put these onto the wires. Positive is red, you can figure out the rest."

Izzy studied the circular lumps of metal in her hand. Rachel gave her a few seconds, then held out a screwdriver. "It's easy."

After fumbling with them for a minute or so, Izzy tightened the screws back down and held up her work.

"Good job. Now, we've got to attach them to the battery. Gonna need a spanner for that."

Rake grumbled and started to snore. Rachel laughed as he dribbled on himself. After a few minutes, Izzy nudged her and pointed to the set-up

"Right." She said. "If everything is working, you should be able to flick the switch on the inverter…"

Izzy pointed to it.

"That's the one."

She put it in the on position, and several green lights flashed to life.

"Congratulations, Izz-illa. You now have a working electrical system."

"Thanks, Starsy." She grinned, handing the tools back. "Now, I heard mention of tea?"

"Yep. Lemme go get everything. Might as well turn that off 'til we're ready to go, don't wanna drain the battery. The kettle will do that in no time..."

Rachel dug through several boxes in the crew-cab of her van, and eventually returned with one filled with cups, tea bags, sugar, and fresh milk. She slid it into Izzy's Defender with a frown. "Might be best to keep this covered up... hadn't considered it before, but other people might want this stuff without asking first. I'm gonna be donating a bunch of stuff I found, so hopefully, that'll keep people from thieving off one another, but better to be on the safe side, right?"

"You're giving it away?"

Rachel nodded. "Yeah. I can't use all of it before it goes out of date. Plus, I'm hoping to convince the others to come with me once they see what I found. Maybe set up a team to help me clear routes and run salvage." She motioned to Stan and McTavish. "Besides, they won't be the only ones out here looking for somewhere to stay. Maybe we can connect to other survivor groups, then figure out how to deal with this properly."

"Sounds like you've given this a lot of thought." Izzy half-filled the kettle, plugged it into the inverter and hit the switch. After a few seconds, a familiar rumbling filled the rear of the Defender.

"When you're out on the motorway, nothing but your thoughts and dead people for company?" She frowned. "You get some time to think."

"So…" Izzy replied, trying to veer the conversation away from the morbid. "When you get your team together, then what?"

"Team or not, I'm still going for London. There might be an evacuation plan going on down there, most populated city in the U.K. right? So it might be the focus of an international aid effort or something."

The kettle clicked off. Izzy carefully poured out three cups before setting it back down.

Rachel nodded to the inverter. "Best to switch it off whenever you're not using it."

"Oh. Yeah. Right."

The whine of a tiny fan died with the flick of the switch.

"Gotta keep on top of that. Until you've got some way to charge it, this is all the power you've got. Kettles and heaters drain it quick, too. And you wanna make sure you don't drain it too much. Damages them, although the inverter should beep before then."

"You're gonna write all this down too?"

Rachel laughed. "Yeah, yeah. Sure. Sorry, this is… I enjoy working with this stuff, right? So I tend to get a bit carried away."

"As you said, I need to be aware of it." Izzy sighed. "Can I get more power?"

"Well… yeah. Sort of. More batteries mean more time before needing to recharge, but your priority should really be finding a charger or solar panels. Hell, a wind turbine is better than nothing."

Izzy squeezed the teabags out and dumped them in an empty cup. "Any ideas where I can find that stuff?"

Rachel shrugged. "Before all this shit, I'd of said rooftops. But from what I've seen, ain't a single building still got a roof.

Some caravans had solar systems, but again, they didn't hold up so good. You're just gonna have to get out there and search around. And that stuff comes with its own set of rules too. When you disconnect solar panels, for example, you wanna make sure they're covered until you plug 'em back in again. Unless of course they're connected to a charge controller, then it doesn't matter so much."

Izzy kicked Rake awake and handed him one of the cups. He glanced at her confused, then took it and peered at the familiar coloured liquid inside. He nodded his thanks and gave it a careful sip.

"Look, if it makes you feel any better, just bring any equipment you find to me, and I'll show you how to set it up, then you can do the rest, right?"

Izzy offered her a relieved smile. "Thanks, Starsy. I dunno what I'd do without you."

"Just stay alive. I don't wanna be responsible for giving you the keys to your own coffin."

Izzy shook her head. "Anchor is a coffin. This Defender? It's freedom."

"Freedom to roam a cage, Iz', until help arrives, we're trapped in the U.K. Don't forget that."

Izzy's gaze drifted towards the entrance, her hands wrapped around the steaming cup in an attempt to warm up. "You know… I was keeping an eye out earlier. Didn't see a single plane. You'd of thought they'd of sent someone to sweep the place. Where are our American or European friends?"

"Who knows?" Rachel shrugged, sipping her tea. "Probably in the same boat we are."

6 - Storm - Reilly The Scavenger

The wind thrashing against Reilly's high-sided van eased as she pulled into the Nissen hut connected to Kelvedon Hatch. The arching metal structure rattled. The few overgrown vines and weeds holding it together strained, but held firm. She came to a stop as close to the end of the tunnel as she felt comfortable, then hurriedly jumped out.

"Keep coming!" She shouted, waving her arms about. At the opening, a large armoured truck revved and lurched forward. Reilly cringed as metal scratched against metal but continued to do what she could to guide them.

As the monstrous engine rattled to a stop, Reilly approached the poorly repaired door leading into the bunker proper. She gave it a loud knock, then turned back to watch the soldiers disembark. There was a thud, then the door swung open. Katie stepped back. "Welcome home."

"Good to be back. Hope you don't mind, but I brought some friends."

Katie frowned. "Did they bring their own food and water too?"

"I managed to find some, but that's neither here nor there." She motioned to someone standing outside and waved them in. "Come on, you're letting all the heat out."

Katie's eyes widened as she saw the uniforms. "You found the army?"

"Yep!" Reilly smiled. "There's a whole bunker North of here. King's Lynn."

"Nice! So we're gonna be rescued?"

Reilly shook her head. "No, that's not why they're here. And any civvie's that turn up at their base are getting sent elsewhere. No, they're here to repair the radio, give medical aid, get an idea of our inventory to see if we need topping up."

As the last of the group came through and dispersed into the bunker, Reilly pulled the door shut.

Katie's shoulders slumped. "We're here for the long haul? What about international help?"

Reilly shrugged. "They haven't been able to make contact with anyone outside the U.K."

"So that's it then? We're on our own?"

"Not exactly. See, King's Lynn reckon they've made contact with a whole bunch of people within the country. And the soldiers kept talking about how many bunkers there really are. Good chance we can band together, you know? Try to rebuild."

Katie stood for a few seconds, rubbing her chin. Eventually, she fixed Reilly with a stare. "Next time you go out, can I come with you?"

Reilly shrugged. "Sure. Why?"

"You're right. We should be working together. I'm gonna find a working vehicle and try and find these 'other places'."

"Alright. Sure. But you'll have to help me with scavenging too. We're not just going out there to hook something up and bring it back here, the bunker's got other needs."

Katie nodded energetically. "Of course. When are you next going?"

"Get some rest tonight. Head out in the morning."

"You come to get me?"

Reilly nodded. "Will do. Before you go running off though, you mind helping me with what I found today?"

"Sure. Anything exciting?"

"Not really. Most of it goes out of date next week too." She pulled the door back open and stepped out to her van. Katie followed her round to the other side. Reilly was already at the side hatch, pulling plastic boxes out and dumping them in the limited space around her.

Katie picked one up, expecting it to be heavier. "What's this? Bread?"

"Yeah. Here." Reilly put another box on top and nodded. "Just stick it inside, we'll sort it all out later."

After a few trips back and forth, Reilly slammed the side door shut once more and helped Katie with the final few boxes. "You still had some in there."

"Yeah. But since we don't have a fridge here, a cold vehicle will have to do. It's just stuff like bacon and pork chops. Don't worry. I'll share."

Katie raised her hands. "I wasn't- I didn't mean…" She sighed. "You don't have to share any of this with anyone, but I'm really thankful you do. I just thought you'd forgotten is all."

"Ah. Nah. Keeping it cool. Maybe tomorrow we can find a caravan and pilfer the fridge from that." She thumb pointed back to her van. "That thing will practically freeze overnight anyway, so might as well make use of it."

"Evening ladies!" Harry called out. He stopped as he saw the boxes, and grinned. "Great work, Ri'!"

"Ah! Just in time!" She replied. "Here." Reilly dropped a box in his hands, then another on top.

"You got one more?"

Reilly shook her head. "You gotta make it down the stairs. No need to show off now, macho man."

"Aw, I'm glad you care."

Reilly stuck out her tongue. "More worried about the food, actually."

With everyone loaded up, they trudged through the damp, by the spluttering pump, down the stairs, and into the mess hall. They were greeted by several survivors who stopped their card games to help. As they took Reilly's boxes, she caught sight of two soldiers talking to the bunker tour guide. He was red-faced and trying to argue, but they didn't seem to pay him much attention as they carried out their inspection and brought things to his attention.

"Getting sick of that guy," Katie said. "Acting like he owns the place."

"He probably feels like he does," Reilly replied. "Spent most of his adult life down here no doubt."

"Just wish he'd try to help more, instead of just bossing people about."

"Maybe that's how he helps? He wants to be careful arguing with the army though. They're here to help, but if he makes it more trouble than it's worth, they'll leave us for more grateful people."

"Ugh. Maybe we should stop him?"

"They don't seem too fussed, to be honest. Sounds like he's getting more of an ear-bashing than they are."

Someone behind one of the counters waved them over. "You want something to eat?"

Reilly nodded. "Yes, please. I'm starving."

"What you want?"

"Toast? And a cup of tea."

"What about you?"

Katie shrugged. "Same as her?"

"Alright. Three minutes. I'll bring it over."

They meandered to an empty table, grabbing sugar and stirrers on the way. As promised, a few minutes later saw them presented with a small meal and something to wash it down with. They sat in silence, the low murmur of the other survivors just enough to drown out the arguments between the soldiers and their host.

Katie pushed her empty plate to one side and relaxed back as much as the bench would allow. "Still feel hungry…"

"Yeah, but we've got to make this last, and we ain't the only ones need feeding."

"I know that, but still… If we're malnourished, we won't function properly, won't think straight. Could lead to bigger problems."

"You know my trick?"

Katie shook her head.

"I have my 'dinner', then I clean up, go to sleep, then get breakfast and go out to wear myself out so I can do it all over again."

"Yeah, but I bet you eat while you're out there too."

"Maybe the odd packet of crisps that floats my way, but not really. People here need it as much as I do, and if we're gonna put things back together, we're gonna need all the help we can get." She tapped her temple. "Playing the long game."

Katie frowned. "I see…"

"And as much as I enjoy sitting around, chatting, this grime isn't going to clean itself off, so…" She got to her feet. "I'll catch you in the morning."

"Yeah, enjoy your shower."

* * *

Reilly unwrapped the damp shirt from her head and tossed it onto the makeshift bed. She'd settled up in a closet near the door, preferring to stay close to her van and away from the other residents. The peace and quiet allowed her time to think and sleep.

She sat down on the edge of the bed and pulled her hair up into a bun. After wiping her hands on the jogging bottoms she'd salvaged, Reilly reached for a book on the overturned crate she was using as a bedside table. She wriggled back on the bed and thumbed through the book until she came to a page with the corner folded over.

* * *

A knock on the door stirred Reilly from her sleep. She wiped the dribble from her mouth and glanced down, the book still open on her chest.

"Reilly? It's Katie. They want to know if you've got anything we need to use today?"

Reilly sat up, rubbing her forehead. "Uhh. Yeah! Gimme a minute!"

She found a pair of clean enough trousers in the pile and pulled them over her nightwear. After redoing her hair, Reilly grabbed her coat, slipped into her trainers, and stepped through the door.

Katie was standing in the corridor. "Uh, morning."

"Morning. Come on, let's go get that bacon. Should bring it all in I suppose… Need the space."

Katie nodded. "Lead the way."

As Reilly stepped out into the crisp morning air, she realized the army truck had gone. "Where're the soldiers?"

Katie waved a hand. "They left early. Couldn't fix the radio so they're bringing us a new one."

The side door slid open with the sound of well-oiled runners. Reilly scanned through a couple of boxes, then pulled two out.

"Good of them. It'll be nice to have the army to call on in times of need."

"From the sounds of it, they've got plenty of people to worry about. Themselves included..."

Reilly nodded. "Yeah, I got that impression."

"It's good news. At least I think it is. One of them was telling me about all the bunkers in London alone." She offered Reilly a hope-filled smile. "If they had enough warning, maybe some of my friends and family survived!"

Reilly closed her eyes and inhaled. "I hope so. But... well... don't get too attached to the idea. It's a real mess out there Kate'. Think about how many people live in the area local to this bunker..." She shrugged. "And we're the only ones to make it here and survive? I've tried to put it out of my mind. Deal with each situation, and if I find someone I know, great, but if not, I'm too preoccupied with something else to let my mind fester."

"I-" Katie frowned. "I need the hope."

"Even so, you gotta take it a step at a time. First step, make sure you're surviving." Reilly passed one of the boxes over and slid the door shut. "Once you can keep yourself fed, watered, and have a roof over your head, then you can turn your attention outward."

"The apocalypse according to Reilly the Scavenger."

Reilly grinned, scooping up the other box and motioning to the bunker door.

"Yeah, I suppose it is. Step two, expand your hunting grounds. The local area won't be able to sustain us for long, so we need vehicles to go farther. The other side of that though..."

Katie pushed through the door. "Hmm?"

"Well... instead of focusing on vehicles so we can salvage the limited resources, we could also be trying to set up a farm or something. Maybe even send people fishing and hunting? We need renewable resources."

"Is that feasible though? What if this happens again?"

Reilly exhaled. "I've been thinking the same thing. Can't risk resettling the surface or sending people out until we're sure."

"But we can't stay underground either."

"Catch twenty-two for sure. Stay and starve, or risk death trying to stay fed. Exactly why we need to take it step by step. And each step we do take, we need to... uhh, what's the word? Fortify it? Like we need to ensure when we move on to the next thing, the stuff we've already set up doesn't fall apart."

They arrived at the mess-hall to a crowd of hungry-eyed

survivors. Some of them cheered at the sight of more food, others, it seemed, didn't have the energy.

"Damn..." Katie muttered. "Stockroom is full, but that guide has us all on a Cold War rationing policy."

"People might be hungry, but they ain't starving. For once he's actually doing the right thing here."

"I don't like seeing people like this. It's hard. Before all this, we were eating well, now it's a struggle to survive and you can see that will-to-survive draining from them."

Reilly set her box down and tapped the lid before one of the self-appointed cooks whisked it away. "As long as there are little bonuses like this every now and then, I think they'll keep going."

"What do we do when the bacon goes off though?"

"Then we move on to cereal, then after that, breakfast bars, then tinned goods. We're not gonna be eating like this forever, granted, but as long as we follow the progression of foods going out of date, I reckon we'll survive long enough to establish a reliable supply."

"Assuming the fish and birds haven't also been killed en-masse by the weather." Katie slid her box onto the counter and turned to an empty table. "I wonder how people would have survived down here after three months? Like what was the government's plan?"

"No clue," Reilly replied, following her. "It takes longer than that for radiation to bugger off."

"Maybe, like us, they thought someone would come to rescue them? Or they could move elsewhere?"

Reilly shrugged. "No clue. Would be nice to figure it out though, might be something we can use."

Katie's stomach rumbled loudly as the smell of smoked bacon wafted through the mess-hall. "Ughhh."

"Easy. It'll be here soon."

Katie fixed her with a frown. "I don't know how you can be so relaxed about all this."

Reilly grinned. "I'm still breathing. That's all that matters."

"I wish I could see it like that. I just keep thinking of all the little things we need to do. It just feels like we're fighting off the inevitable."

"Nah. Can't think like that." Reilly pointed to the door. "Millions of people have come before and will come after. Plenty of civilizations have fallen to dust only for the remnants to repopulate the world, this is just one of those. We're the survivors, Kay', we're the ones who are gonna rebuild. And when you look at it from that perspective instead, it becomes more interesting. You know the Chinese have the same word for crisis and opportunity?"

"Just think of everything we had though. Do you remember central heating? Computers? Smartphones? All of humanity's achievements reduced to rubble."

"Jeez', you're starting to make me feel glum. Let's just put a pin in this conversation for now. Wait till you see it with your own eyes. Maybe then you'll see the potential." She scooted back as one of the cooks brought over a tray and laid it in front of the pair with a cheeky smile. Upon it sat two paper cups filled with tea, a mess of sugars, stirrers, milk, and two plates with a bacon sandwich on each. Reilly thanked him as Katie scooped hers up and began eating.

"Oh." She said between chewing. "This is gooooood."

Reilly grinned then picked up her own. "You know, you should save some for lunch."

"I don't think that's going to happen." She swallowed. "Do you?"

"Ha. I guess not. Remember though, we can't go eating all the stuff we find. If we get hungry out there, we can't betray these people by eating the stuff we're supposed to be bringing them. And if we're obviously eating better than they are, people might get upset."

"To be honest, I thought you were eating stuff anyway and just accepted it. You're the one risking your neck out there, so what if you eat? More people should have grabbed vehicles and gone searching."

"Which would probably lead to people fighting one another for resources." Reilly shook her head. "Nah, need to think more long-term."

They enjoyed the rest of their meal listening to the conversations on surrounding tables. The mood had lifted considerably with breakfast, and some people were even laughing and joking. Reilly slid her plate back onto the tray, knocked back the last of her tea, then got to her feet.

"You ready?"

Katie nodded. "Yep. Let's go."

On the way out, they were stopped by a couple of people and offered thanks. Reilly returned smiles and encouragements before finally escaping into the corridor. The smells from the mess-hall had woken the late-sleepers, and it was something of a struggle to navigate the crowd. Eventually, though, Reilly and Katie arrived at the van and climbed in.

"Er." Katie said, hovering over the passenger seat.

"Oh. Sorry." Reilly grabbed the pile of maps and notepads and tossed them in the back. Katie sat down and quickly got comfortable.

"A real seat! I'd almost forgotten what they felt like. Those benches are horrible."

"No kidding. I wouldn't get too comfortable though, gonna be in and out most of the day." She started the engine and rolled the window down.

Katie glanced to the side mirror as they began backing out.

"I'm looking forward to it actually. Getting away from the bunker, some fresh air. Fair enough, I'd rather be at home watching YouTube, but this will certainly do given the circumstances."

As they emerged onto the jagged tarmac, Reilly heard Katie's breath catch in her throat. All around them, trees had fallen, electric cables lashed at the rain-soaked surroundings, and pipes had been torn from the ground. Reilly carefully navigated the heaps of earth and other obstacles strewn over the road as Katie regained her composure.

"Pretty bad, eh?" She asked as they pulled up to the main road.

"I didn't think it-" Katie sighed. "We were lucky to be in that bunker."

"Ain't that the truth."

Katie glanced back out the window, lazily scanning the sporadic wrecked vehicles they passed.

"You know..." Reilly continued. "I really thought I was gonna die. The second you guys opened that door though, I've never been so thankful in my life."

"Is that why you give the guide such an easy time? Because he's letting us stay there?"

Reilly scrunched her nose. "I dunno. It's not really his place to say, is it? I mean yeah, technically he's got the most right, but trying to kick out a bunch of people into almost certain death... well, it wouldn't go how he planned."

"I hope it doesn't come to that."

Reilly nodded, relaxing back in her seat. "Yeah. I think the army talked some sense into him though. Like he's more than just the caretaker of the bunker now, he's the caretaker of the people inside too. Think he was still looking at it from the historical preservation side."

Katie blinked. "He was more concerned with the bunker? That… explains a lot actually."

"Right? But now, someone's been able to vocalize what none of us could. It's got him thinking. Ain't no tourists at the end of the world, bunker should be used to protect people."

"Funny how it all comes full-circle."

"What do you mean?"

"Originally, it was built to protect us. Then they turned it into a museum. Now…" Katie drew a circle in their air. "Back to protecting us again."

Reilly smirked. "You know, I hope it can go back to being a museum again. Like… hmm, like I hope we get to live in a world where 'tourists' are a thing again."

"Speaking of tourists, where are we headed?"

"Up the M-eleven. Between here and King's Lynn, there are some services near Bishops Stortford. I'm thinking that's the sort of place that'd have food, and things like torches, air-mattresses. You know, the usual tat they sell at those places."

"Stuff the bunker could use…"

"Spot on."

Reilly became lost in concentration as she weaved through the mess of the motorway. The farther north they traveled, the less consideration had been given to ensuring a clear path. "This is where I met the army," Reilly said, motioning to the mess. "They just pushed through all this… I'd been trying to make it… not neat, but a bit more organized. Oh, and if you come across any cars with their fuel caps out, don't bother. Between me and them, we cleared up this little section, fuel-wise."

"Oh?"

"Yeah. Sadly she doesn't run on will-power, just good ol' diesel."

"Diesel?" Katie hummed. "So it might be an idea for me to get a petrol car?"

Reilly shrugged. "Sure? It's up to you really. Diesel lasts longer, but you can easily find more petrol, so it's a balance I guess. Gotta remember that fuel will go bad eventually too."

"Hmm… fair enough."

They rolled up the off-ramp and into more traffic. This time, a lorry sat at a precarious angle between the roundabout and the junction exit. Reilly cautiously worked her way around it, then pulled onto another road. A blue sign with the word 'Services' written on it banged about in the wind. They followed the long winding road, first to a large truck car-park that looked more like a scrapyard, then to a split. Another sign, this one barely readable, directed them to the main building.

"Jesus," Katie said as they turned the corner.

Reilly came to a stop and stared out the windscreen, her mouth agape. Ahead of them, a wall of vehicles had been pushed into the surrounding grass verges, creating a mangled barrier of twisted metal and seat cushions, sitting in a pool of oil, coolant, and fuel. To the left, several walls of the services still stood, held up by more displaced vehicles.

"Let's just get this done." Katie finally said. "This place is freaking me out."

Reilly shook herself from the daze and nodded. "Yes. Right. Uhh… Let's leave the van here, go grab what we can, and drag it back here. I don't see any way through all this."

Katie nodded. "Me either."

Reilly turned the key, zipped up her coat, and opened the door. A sudden gust almost ripped it out of her hand, but she held firm and made it outside.

"Weather's getting worse!" Katie shouted.

"Then we better hurry!"

They fought against the growing gale and light drizzle and made it to the entrance. Reilly didn't hesitate, getting on her hands and knees to crawl through a broken floor-level window. Katie reluctantly followed. As she got to her feet and brushed herself off, she glanced around. The light from Reilly's torch bounced from crumbling ceiling to overturned magazine racks, to fallen arcade machines. Apart from the glass crunching underfoot, the only sound that could be heard was the growing wind.

"Where are all the people?" Katie asked as they reached the main shopping area.

"Best not to think about it. The important thing is, we ain't trudging through a mountain of bodies to get what we want."

"Still though… lot of cars out there. You think they survived? Moved somewhere else?"

"I don't know what to think." Reilly started towards one of the shops, the shutter half down. "And I reckon the more we try to figure it out, the more we're gonna uncover answers we don't like. What if you found out that the management locked the doors and turned everyone away? Left all those people in their vehicles or trying to outrun what was happening." She ducked under the shutter and began poking around the counter.

"I hope that isn't the case, but still… I don't like unanswered questions. What if they come back? What if we're looting their home? Imagine if someone went to the bunker while we were out and took all the stuff we had."

Reilly pulled a packet of sturdy bags from behind the counter, split it, and passed a couple over to Katie. "Wouldn't happen. We've always left people behind. Besides, this place isn't a bunker, it hasn't held up well enough to be safe."

"Another reason to ask questions," Katie replied, shaking a bag open and moving closer to the fridges. "What if they abandoned it because of a gas leak? Or an electrical fault?"

"Just be careful, mindful of what you're doing." Reilly began filling her bag with batteries, candles, and travel goods. When she reached bursting point, Reilly moved over to the food section. She studied the fridges, then the aisle food, then decided her bounty was in the fruit section.

With several full bags between them, Reilly rejoined Katie at the door and the two of them made their escape. They could hear the wind whistling near the entrance.
"We should hurry. Sounds like the weather is making a return visit."

Reilly squeezed through the window. A gust of wind stumbled her as she got to her feet, but after a few seconds of fighting it, Reilly found her footing. She pulled the bags through and kept a firm grip on the handles. Her knuckles turning white, so desperate was she to keep hold of their prizes.
"Come on!" She yelled, urging Katie to her feet. "Let's go!"

They struggled through the wind and rain that battered them. Reaching the van, Reilly called out. "Side door!"
Despite the small surface area, a gust still caught the sliding door. It flew out of Katie's hand and slammed to a stop on its rails. Reilly pushed the loot in, then helped Katie inside. Once she'd found somewhere to grip the door, she forced it back despite the winds protests.

Katie glanced up at her from the floor. "Thank you."

Reilly dropped into the driver's seat and started the engine. "You okay?"

"I'll live. Question is, are we gonna be alright?"

"If I've got anything to say about it."

Reilly slammed the van into reverse, turned the wheel, and began rolling back the way they'd come. She could feel the wind beating against them, and it took all of her concentration just to keep it under control The van skidded in the rain, but Reilly encouraged it. Once they were facing the right direction again, she gripped the gear-stick, put it into first, and pressed the accelerator. She leaned forward, squinting through the sideways rain, trying to remember where the clear path had been.

Reilly barely noticed when Katie squeezed through the gap between their seats and sat down.

"Anything I can do to help?"

"Uhh… not really. Keep an eye out."

"Alright. Remember that truck up the end here."

"Got it."

After about half an hour of precarious driving, Reilly snapped out of her concentration trance and glanced up. She began laughing. "Look! Clear skies!"

Katie leaned forward. "We made it?"

"I hadn't even realized. Guess we outran it."

"What even was it?" Katie adjusted her seat and relaxed back. "You reckon it's happening again?"

Reilly shook her head. "No… The first time it was sudden, right? Unexpected. This… well, look." She motioned to the sky. "This is coming on slowly. Sure, it's pretty strong, but not like before."

"I hope you're right. Still though, gonna be hard to rebuild on the surface with weather like this."

"Hopefully it'll pass. If not, then we might have to think about making the bunk-"

Katie sat up in her seat suddenly and waved her hand. "Hold up!"

"What's…?" Reilly followed her sightline. Ahead of them, a red sports four by four sat by the side of the road, precariously hanging over the edge. "Seriously?"

"Let's take a look." Her face reddened. "And uh, sorry. I didn't mean to interrupt you."

"All good."

The van came to a stop and Katie jumped out. Reilly left the engine running and joined her. There was a harsh chill in the air. She saw Katie's breath, then glanced to the vehicle. "Huh." She said. "Honda. HR-V. Jap' cars tend to be pretty reliable. And if memory serves, this should be a petrol."

Katie cautiously approached and peered through the window. "No-one in here, either. Still got the key. Guess the driver got blown away... or something." She shivered.

"Well look... It's probably the best we're gonna find. Let's just get it towed, get back to the bunker before that storm comes in."

Katie stepped back and nodded. "Alright, how are we doing this?"

"I've got some tow-line. You hook up this side, I'll attach it to the van, then once it's back on solid ground, you steer it through this mess."

"I'll be in this all the way back to the Hatch?"

Reilly nodded. "Yeah, we can pull it, but we can't steer it from the van."

She hurried back to her vehicle, pulled open one of the back doors, seized a grease-covered strap and jogged back to Katie.

"Here. Just hook it on at the back there. I'll pull it out, then we can put it on the front."

The metal hooks clipped into place with a satisfying clunk. Once Reilly was happy they were secure, she climbed back into the van and began gently pulling forward. She could barely hear Katie's directions as the engine revved.

"Okay! Stop there!"

Reilly watched Katie unhook the Honda and open the door.

"All the windows are intact, and…" She leaned in and gave the keys a turn. The engine sprung to life instantly.

Reilly started laughing. "You're kidding me?"

"Apparently not…"

"Well, in that case, I'll follow you."

"Follow me? Why?"

"Well if you break down and I'm in front, might not hear or see it. This way, I can keep an eye on things."

Katie nodded. "Alright. Good thinking."

Reilly motioned to the darkness on the horizon. "That storm is definitely coming this way. Come on."

They got into their respective vehicles. Katie promptly sped past Reilly with a grin on her face. Reilly couldn't help but laugh as she put her foot down and followed after her.

"Nice one."

When no reply came, Reilly suddenly felt a pang of loneliness. Her thoughts drifted to King's Lynn, and the soldiers there.

At least we're not completely alone out here…

Leaning forward, she clicked the radio on and settled in for the journey.

7 - Project - Tina Reyes

Looking out over the sodden ground, Colonel Tina Reyes groaned and peeled her gloves off. She was stood by the entrance to the bunker, watching as soldiers ran supplies back and forth, or tried pushing vehicles back onto their wheels.

"Takes quite a force to roll a Foxhound."

Reyes turned to look at Ross Niles. "Yes, sir."

"However, this doesn't look like the same level of damage we experienced during the first strike. Would you agree with my assessment that the storm is weakening?"

She glanced at the remains of the care home that had once hidden the bunker entrance. "It is my assessment that a lot of the damage had already been done. Although, the weather anomaly only forced us to take shelter for the night instead of a few days."

"Do we have any way of tracking it?" Niles asked, rubbing his chin.

"Private Edwards has been able to get a rough idea by the level of interference from the radio station broadcasting out there."

"Oh?"

"The host keeps giving his co-ordinates out. By listening to the level of interference on that frequency, Private Edwards is able to estimate a very rough location of the storm."

"There's only one station we can do this with?"

"It's the only consistent one. Charlie and Delta switch off distress broadcasts as they find them, and the radios we provided to the nearby bunkers aren't in use frequently enough. Private Edwards doesn't think they'd be much of a warning either due to their proximity."

"Too close to work as a meaningful early warning system?"

Reyes nodded. "Yes, sir."

"Very well," Niles replied. "Keep me updated."

"There is one thing, sir."

"Yes?"

"We've been receiving a lot of distress signals from the North Sea, but they go quiet shortly after transmission. We believe a vessel or fleet of vessels has survived and is assisting survivors, but have no evidence either way as of yet."

"If that is the case, I'm glad I'm here and not out there. Let me know if Edwards comes up with anything further."

As he turned back to the entrance, Reyes spoke up again.

"Sir, Charlie team have returned."

Niles looked over to the road. "I don't see…"

Reyes tapped her ear and smiled. In the distance, she could hear the roar of the Cromwell and the snapping of tree-trunks. "In the future, I will be more mindful of the location of the storm before I send teams out."

"You could have done worse than send them to RAF Marham," Reyes replied. "There are some extremely sturdy buildings there."

"Hopefully something we can use. I look forward to their report."

He descended out of sight as the top half of a tree rolled past the remnants of the gate. The sound of the convoy grew, and Reyes felt a shiver of excitement as the first of the vehicles appeared. Dans was standing through one of the tank's hatches, he cheered as they crossed the threshold.

"You can celebrate after you've given your report, Lieutenant."

"Uh, ah." He straightened up. "Yes, ma'am!"

"Easy. Just hoping you bought some of that extra morale for everyone."

"Ahh… I'm just happy to be home, ma'am, but I think everyone will be pleasantly surprised."

"I hope so." She glanced up at the convoy as they looked for somewhere to park. "Where's Lance Corporal Warwick?"

"In the fuel truck. We found it at Marham."

Reyes smiled. "That is a pleasant surprise. When you're finished parking, find him and present yourselves to the Major General."

"Yes, ma'am!"

She watched as the rest of the vehicles lined up neatly and shut their engines off. The convoy numbered nineteen, a mix of armored cars, tanks, and trucks, all coated in mud and dust. Reyes could feel the buzz of excitement in the air as the soldiers jumped out and began unloading equipment.

A couple hauling a crate stomped by on their way to the entrance, then stopped. Reyes glanced over. "Problem?"

"Where are we taking these, ma'am?"

"What have you got?"

"M.R.E's, ma'am."

"And everyone else?"

"Weapons, fuel, generators, medical supplies, other support

equipment."

She raised her voice as if to address everyone. "Food goes to the mess hall. Weapons and military equipment are to be checked in at the cage. All medical equipment goes to our med-bay. The rest goes into dry storage. I also hope to see some meticulous record-keeping regarding what you picked up." She looked back to the pair hauling the crate. "Anything else?"

"No, ma'am. Thank you."

She grinned. "No, thank you. These supplies will keep the bunker going a few more weeks at least."

As the flurry of work went on around her, Reyes' eye was drawn to the road. She heard the revving of an engine, then a bang as it backfired. She motioned to Dans and Lefty, who quickly fell in behind her as she cautiously made her way towards the gate.

The pained rumble of the engine grew louder. Reyes squinted. In the distance, growing larger with every passing second, she could make out the lumbering frame of a coach as it rocked and rolled over the destroyed road towards the bunker.

For less than a second, Reyes closed her eyes as her mind raced with a thousand images all at once. Looking down, she saw herself holding her service rifle and wearing tac-gear. Sand swirled around mud huts, the sun-baked her skin. Across from her, another soldier waved a van through their makeshift checkpoint. Her attention snapped to a crossroads farther down. Reyes heard the growing rumble of an engine. It revved loudly, metal scratched against the brick. She tried screaming to her team, but no words came out. She raised her rifle as a truck smashed through a building on the corner and continued its unrelenting charge towards the group.

Reyes could feel her legs moving under her, then a thud as she smashed into another soldier, knocking him clear just as the truck wing mirror knocked her to the dirt.

Reyes opened her eyes and turned to Dans, focused and alert. "E.T.A. forty seconds. Can you block it?"

He didn't answer. Instead, Dans and Lefty both moved at lightning speed back to the row of vehicles and piled into the tank. A bead of sweat ran down Reyes' forehead as the coach got closer. The noise of the damaged engine now fought against the unforgiving sound of the Cromwell, and it was losing. Mud sprayed Reyes as the tank pulled into position and leveled the turret on the incoming coach.

The next few seconds were a blur for Reyes. The first thing she heard was the loud screeching of the coach's brakes. Then the hissing of hydraulics as the whole thing came to an abrupt halt, tearing up tarmac and cement. Several of the tyres exploded, causing it to tilt lazily to the left. It began skidding to one side on metal rims.

Reyes snapped back to reality and called out to Dans, "Idiot! Go help!"

As the tank roared off, she turned back to the rest of the soldiers. Some had grabbed the weapons from their latest mission, while others had picked up stretchers and med-packs.

Luke Warwick tossed Reyes a rifle and nodded to her. "What's the plan?"

"Follow me. Anyone without a weapon holds back until we've secured the vehicle."

She started towards the coach. The sound of metal grinding

against metal filled the air as the tank propped it up.

Reyes motioned for Luke to take a small group and head around the far side. He nodded, pulling several people to his side before they broke off from Reyes' team. Both groups circled the vehicle, trying to hold back coughing as they passed through clouds of exhaust smoke and dust.

Over the sound of everything else, Reyes heard Luke shouting that he was ready. She approached the front passenger door and watched as her team took their positions. Reyes shouted back that she was ready. "Breach on three! One-two-three!"

The glass in the door shattered as two burly men slammed it open. As soon as there was an opening, two more piled in, followed by Reyes, who was then followed by the opening team. She passed an unconscious driver, a trickle of blood ran from a fresh head wound and his breathing seemed uneven. She pressed forward and found herself looking into the faces of at least twenty terrified people. They wore torn clothes, and through the mud and dirt, wore confused, angry and fearful expressions.

"Jesus," Luke said, joining her in the aisle. "What a mess."

"We need to get these people out of here," Reyes replied.

"Find the least wounded, get them out. I'll bring up the medics." She passed the door-openers, pulling them to one side. "Watch them. They might be wounded, and they sure look like civilians, but I'm leaving nothing to chance now." Her expression hardened. "Remember, we've only got the one bunker."

Reyes stepped off the coach and through the smoke once more to see Ross waiting for her. "Would you mind explaining what's going on?"

She waved to the other soldiers to move up then fixed him with a stare. "Incoming vehicle. Intentions unclear. Blocked the entrance with the tank. Coach came to a quick stop, resulting in the damage. Ordered tank to assist coach while we now aid what appears to be civilians."

Niles glanced to the straining tank, then to the leaning coach and frowned. "Do you have the situation under control?"

She shook her head. "No. But I'm working on it, sir."

"Very well." He stepped back as a dazed woman stumbled towards him. A couple of medics flanked her on either side and carried her closer to the bunker before sitting her down on the road.

Reyes directed the other survivors down the road and into the arms of the others. Luke came out after, carrying a bruised and blood-covered woman over his shoulder.

"Eight left." He said. "Including the driver."

"Any of them-"

"Not yet, ma'am," Luke replied quickly. "Most are still in shock."

Reyes' shoulders slumped. "Alright. Carry on."

She wandered over to the tank and considered giving the back panel a smack to get their attention, then worried that Dans would misconstrue it as a sign to get out of the way.

"Stay where you are, we're almost done unloading. I repeat, stay where you are!"

She heard a sharp tap and took it as a sign that they'd heard her.

Turning back, she saw a truck emerging from the bunker complex. It pulled up just shy of her and several people jumped out with ropes and chains. They directed the truck into position, then set about rigging up the coach. Luke shouted over that they were all clear, and the tow team quickly set to work.

Reyes wandered through the battered and bruised survivors, looking for someone copacetic enough to talk to. Eventually, she found a shivering teenager smoking a cigarette and trying to comfort his friend. She pulled him to one side and spoke quietly.

"Who are you? And why are you here?"

He tugged his arm away. "Get your hands off of me, lady. We're from Coltishall. This was the only other safe place we knew about."

"It's not open to civilians," Reyes replied bluntly.

"So what? You're just gonna force us into the storm? Come on, lady, you gotta help us."

"I don't have to do anything. You came charging at us and now you-"

"Yeah, and look where it got us. Everyone gets a free concussion and a limp because they came asking for help. Some worse. Plus, you just destroyed the one vehicle that might have taken us away from here. It'd be pretty shitty of you to abandon us now."

"Abandon you? We never asked you to come here in the first

place. In fact, we've been giving pretty clear instructions to the contrary. Now your plan has backfired you're trying to make me feel bad?"

"We didn't come here to leech off you army fuckheads. A lot of the people you almost just killed are engineers, architects, people who have a potential solution to what's happening out here. We came here because we can't do it without your help."

Reyes smirked, disbelieving. "You know how to stop the storm?"

"No. But we know about the Wangford Cement Quarry. It's over a hundred meters deep, containers are eight feet tall, that's almost forty floors. We want to build a bunker, one that can handle the storm, one that we can build quickly using supplies from nearby ports. One large enough to support any number of potential survivors."

Reyes studied him for a moment, her mind raced with all the potential problems of such a project, but the glimmer in his eyes was something she hadn't seen for a few days; hope.

"I'm probably going to regret this." Reyes started. "But... find your brightest minds, and, if they're able, join me at the bunker entrance."

"You're seriously going to hear us out?"

"Not me. Major General Ross Niles." She sighed. "Look, I don't know if this is even feasible, but it's something. I appreciate it's easier to complain than fix the problem, so I respect that you're trying, but this sounds big. Don't get your hopes up."

"No offense, lady, but this is the only chance we've got. The coach was only ever going to bring us this far, and with no bunker to go back to, we're as good as dead the moment we start traveling. Either you and your general friend help us, or you kill us. I know which I'd rather have on my conscious."

"Let's get one thing straight, my name is Tina Reyes, you will address me as Colonel, or ma'am. Secondly, I don't know how much faith we should put in engineers who can't keep a coach functional, let alone their own bunker. And thirdly, you chose to come here, there are at least four other bunkers local to here, with another farther south. So no, *boyo,* we aren't the ones who ended you, you did that to yourself, we're just your last lifeline, and if I were you, I'd start treating us with some respect."

"After what you did to my friends?"

"Your driver did that. And like I said, you didn't even have to come here. We broadcast very clearly that this area is for military personnel only. No civilians, even desperate ones with extreme plans. Just be thankful that I'm giving you a chance to speak to the Major General."

He frowned. "Yeah, thanks a bunch."

"Go find your people, then meet me at the entrance. Maximum of four, including yourself."

He shrunk away without another word. Reyes saw the Cromwell emerge from a smoke cloud and pull up just shy of the gate. Dans poked his head through the hatch and glanced around at all the chaos.

"Ah… uh, I'm assuming that could have gone better…"

Reyes bit her lip and closed her eyes. "Dans. I don't have the mental capability to deal with you right now. But I want you to know that I am extremely angry."

"Uh… yes, ma'am."

"Get rid of the tank then help everyone else fix the mess that you caused."

"We weren't going to fire!" Dans protested. "We haven't any ammo, ma'am."

"And how were they supposed to know it's just for show? Especially when it's pointed right at them? Now, I gave you an order and I swear to god-"

"Yes ma'am, going ma'am."

The tank turned on the spot then rolled back into its parking space. Reyes followed behind it, breaking off as she approached the bunker entrance.

Several minutes later she was standing in Ross Niles' office with two people who couldn't stand up properly, and the young smoker she'd spoken to. Her finger hovered around the safety on her rifle.

"I'm sorry?" Niles said, resting his chin on weaved fingers. "Run that by me again."

A man with a thick beard limped forward. Tina noted his skin seemed to hang off slightly as if he were once a chubby man but the lack of food had quickly changed that.

"There's a hole in the ground, one hundred meters deep. Probably half that wide. People have been mining there for decades. Or, quarrying I suppose. Point is, there's a blank canvas there for a bunker." He poked his open palm. "We use the resources there, plus containers from all the docks and harbours around the U.K. Sink 'em into the ground, reinforce the exteriors with cement and steel, That'd be about thirty-five levels. There'd be a huge parking space, generator room, hydroponics gardens, hundreds of apartments for people, a market, hell, whatever you want." His voice strained. "Mostly, it'll be protected."

Niles thought for a moment, then asked, "This is all possible?"

"There are a lot of ifs. Hydroponics labs will require grow lights and seeds, the generator will need constant refueling unless you know where we can dig up a nuclear reactor, and we'll need manpower."

Niles shook his head. "Unfortunately, I think a nuclear reactor is out of reach."

"Actually sir-" Reyes cut in. "If we can make contact with any of our Trident assets, a nuclear reactor might not be such an extreme measure."

"I see… And you think this is a good idea?"

Reyes shook her head. "I think it's an idea, sir. Whether it's a good one remains to be seen."

The bearded man cleared his throat. "And I'd agree with that. We're not blind to how massive this is, but if that storm doesn't fuck off right sharp, we're not going to have any bunkers left. We were flooded out of Coltishall, and anywhere on the surface that's managed to survive this long won't last much longer. We need something."

"I see." Niles unwove his fingers and relaxed back in his chair. "I can't deny that we know very little about the storm. If it fades, will it come back? If it doesn't fade then how are we supposed to deal with it? I also agree that the bunkers we have available to us are in an unfit condition. We can't rely on them for much longer. I also realise that without a government behind us, the decision of moving forward with this project falls to me." He sighed. "But I cannot ignore the obvious fact here; if this fails, time and people-power that could have been used elsewhere would have been wasted, and with our limited resources, that could mean the difference between life and death." He glanced up at Reyes. "Colonel, do you have anything to add?"

"Yes, sir."

He raised his hand, motioning for her to continue.

"Firstly, I would ask for any plans or blueprints so that we can speak to our own engineers. If no such plans exist, I would encourage you to seek out our engineers and work with them to create some. I'd also like to point out that if we do agree to go ahead with this, we're going to want equipment ready to go. If we assemble space for one of these hydroponics gardens, but there are no lights or seeds, then what was the point? And I'd encourage you to focus on resource production first. Having a market might be nice, but it doesn't solve any immediate problems such as food or electricity."

"We'll get you the plans."

"Very well," Niles said, getting to his feet. "Now, we have the small issue of where to put everyone."

"You're letting us stay?"

"The colonel here suggested that if I like what I hear, I might 'recruit' you as advisors. So far, I'm on the fence. You've brought me vague ideas-"

The bearded man drew breath to reply but Niles cut him off.

"But you're also the only ones to do so. So until a better offer presents itself, or we agree to follow through with this, you'll be considered advisors."

The smoker stepped away from the wall with a frown. "What does that mean exactly?"

"It means that you get to live under our roof, but you also have to follow our rules. You'll get two hots and a cot, and if the officer assigned to you asks you to do something, you better do it."

"And if we don't like what we're asked to do?"

"Hm. I see I need to make some things apparent to you." Niles stepped out from behind the desk, everyone but Reyes moved backward. She'd watched him switch from the thoughtful listener to having a commanding presence over the room. "The United Kingdom has been hit by an apocalyptic level weather event. Help isn't coming. I have graciously opened the doors to this military facility because you were incapable of maintaining your own shelter, and you might potentially have a solution. However, I will not hesitate to throw you all back out there if you feel it's too much trouble to mop the floor or cook some meals. If people are going to survive, if this bunker is going to last long enough to realize this scheme of yours, then everybody needs to pull their weight. Am I making myself clear?"

"Crystal."

"Good. Now I'd appreciate it if the three of you left us. Ask the people on the door, nicely, to guide you back to your friends." The bearded man nodded, mumbled a "Yes sir." and ambled out with his companions in tow.

"I can see why you encouraged patience with the young one," Niles said, returning to his seat.

"Hot-headed. But their idea might have merit."

"Which is why I'm sending you and Alpha out to survey the location. This Wangford Quarry."

Reyes tried to hide her grin. "Thank you for the opportunity, sir."

"Primary objective is to assess the area. How difficult would it be to bring supplies in? Are there any pumps? And if so, are they operational? What sort of damage has the storm done?"

Reyes nodded. "You'll have an extremely detailed report by the time I return, sir."

"Good. And while you're doing that, Bravo will be going to Felixstowe to assess how many usable containers are there and how we intend on moving them."

"Should I take some of the 'advisors' with me, sir?"

Niles nodded. "The guy with the beard. Might be an idea to get all their names, too. I'll have Henk and Yasmir take everyone's details when they assign them to a well-guarded space."

"I will assemble the team and head out immediately."

"Good luck."

* * *

It had taken two days to reach Wangford Quarry, and despite a slow and steady approach, the eight vehicles that made up the Alpha team convoy were battered and running low on fuel. Reyes sat in the back of an armoured troop carrier, checking over the list of supplies as they rocked and rolled over the jagged road surface and up to the edge of the quarry.

She glanced to the driver as they came to a stop.

"We're here, ma'am."

"Alright," Reyes replied. She motioned for the person closest to the rear door to open it, and soon the group piled out into the fresh air, stretching and yawning as their feet hit solid ground again.

"Happy to be out of that sweatbox." One person said to a chorus of agreement.

"Alright team, take five, then I want these vehicles refueled."

There was another, less-enthusiastic murmur of agreement.

Tina turned to the bearded man. "Jeff, you're with me, you too, Mike."

"Ma'am?"

"We've got a hole to inspect."

Moving closer to the edge, Reyes felt her breath catch in her throat. "Jesus."

She looked out over the enormous man-made crater dug into the Earth, unable to take it all in at once. A spiral ramp led into a huge, dirty grey lake at the bottom. Several bloated bodies sat on the surface among a myriad of other detritus.

"Reckoned as much," Jeff said, stroking his beard. "See the pipes?" He asked, pointing.

Tina nodded, backing away from the edge. "Yes?"

"Well, they're connected to pumps. If they're still operational... As in, the storm hasn't done too much damage, then we can fire them up and suck that swimming pool dry."

"What about all the deceased down there? And the trees and cars?"

"Storm must have dumped the big stuff down there. Shame it can't lift it back out. No, sorry, I'm afraid that'll be on whatever workforce you send into that hole once we're done pumping."

"I take it you're not volunteering?"

Jeff laughed. "After what your friends did to my leg? You're lucky I'm even here."

"Maybe next time you approach a military facility, you'll go a bit slower."

"Amen to that."

"So what, you turn the pumps back on, we send people down there to clean everything out, then we just start dumping containers down there?"

"That's a crude way of puttin' it, but essentially yeah. Gotta check the foundations, make sure they can support what we're planning. First thing we'd build would be a loading area, somewhere for supplies and people to protect them from the storm. I guess you'd call it a base camp."

"Seeing it with my own eyes…" Reyes trailed off. "It's big. I mean, overwhelmingly so."

"In this case, that's a good thing. The bigger this hole is, the more essentials we can fit down there. We'd only be limited by the number of containers, and the amount of concrete and steel."

Mike finished scribbling in his notepad and turned from the edge to face Jeff. "And the number of cranes and trucks that have survived."

"Well, of course, we'd need equipment, but between the cranes at the docks and roads drowning in trucks, we can pull something together. Especially now we're not worrying about the storm killin' us. Might be a little rough, but hey, it's the apocalypse."

"Thanks, Jeff," Reyes replied. "I hadn't noticed."

"I'm just saying, to get this done, we're gonna have to go proper scrapheap challenge."

Reyes rubbed her forehead and sighed. "Okay, say you sort all that stuff out, what's stopping the storm from rolling through and undoing all our hard work?"

"Well, it'd help if we had a better idea of where the storm was, but we can use reinforcing techniques, increase the power on the pumps… Even setting a schedule for when a secure section is in place, then waiting the storm out before we continue with the next secure bit. Fill the hole as we go, make sure everything is cemented in place so the storm can't move it."

"Sounds like you're throwing lots of half-ideas out."

"Well, until I see the plan our joint team of engineers comes up with, I know as much as you do."

"Mike?" Reyes asked. "What do you think?"

"I think it'll be a big job, ma'am, but I can see the merits of using this place. Half the work has already been done."

"And from an engineering standpoint?"

"I'd like to see how many containers you can stack on one another before it becomes too much, but with the correct reinforcement, it shouldn't even be an issue. I wouldn't have signed off on something like this prior to everything that's happened, but now, I don't see many alternatives."

Reyes looked out over the quarry and sighed. "Alright. Get a team down there and see what we're dealing with." She turned and started back towards the convoy. "I've got a *very* interesting report to write…"

8 - Surface - Ada

On the western outskirts of London, down a thin track of road covered in sporadic tangles of branches and dying plants, Ada crawled through the ruins of the Home Counties Outdoor Centre, dragging a heavy bag behind her. She wore a scarf over her mouth and a pair of scuffed pink ski goggles in an attempt to protect herself from the harsh environment. The air was so thick with dust, she only had the weak flicker of a wind-up torch and the sound of Jack's voice to guide herself to safety.

"Not as easy as you thought, eh?" He called out.

Ada grunted, her voice muffled. "Better than some office job."

"You'd rather crawl about on your hands and knees?"

"Too right!"

Emerging into an opening, Ada slowly raised her hand to check her headspace, then stood up. A row of barred windows let in what little daylight remained. She moved more confidently as her eyes adjusted.

Jack's voice echoed from an open doorway across the room.

"Hurry up, Ade."

"And risk hurting myself? I don't think so!"

"This is the fourth time. You gotta know where it's safe to walk by now."

"The place is literally falling down around my ears. Chill out."

Ada carefully stepped through the opening and saw Jack's flashlight beyond a set of twisted entry doors. She stepped onto an overturned display, ducked under the collapsed portion of the roof, around some broken timbers, then over a pile of bricks before finally squeezing through the pried open doors. Ada tossed the bag onto a pile of others and brushed herself off.

"I hope that was worth it," Jack said coldly.

"You're kidding, right?" She pulled the scarf and goggles off before jamming them into her coat pocket. "This stuff? This is our long-term survival strategy!"

"Really?" Jack wandered over to the pile and picked up a sleeping bag. "What are we going to do with a bunch of sleeping bags, tents and backpacks?"

"Oh, I don't know?" Ada replied. "Maybe trade them for the stuff we do need?"

"Trade with who?"

"Other people, obviously. You heard the radio, there are more like us."

"I need more proof than some lone geriatric."

"Er, alright Captain America, what about me?"

"What about you?"

"I'm proof, aren't I? Before me, you hadn't met anyone."

"And it looks like that trend is set to continue." Jack exhaled, his chest heaved. "Whatever. Let's just load this crap and find somewhere to sleep."

"Look," Ada replied, scooping up one of the bags. "There's more here than just some tents and snooze-bags, right? We've got a bunch of camping meals now, first aid stuff, even some little USB solar panels."

"Oh good, I can charge my cell phone." He pulled open the side door on the Transit and tossed the sleeping bag inside before heading back to the pile.

"Who would you call?"

"I was being sarcastic."

"So was I, but if it's got a torch or a radio on it, MP3 player, that sort of thing…"

"Uhh, Ade, give it a rest. I get it. You couldn't be happier that this has happened, but me? I'm fucking terrified, alright?" He threw another bag into his van and sighed as the suspension creaked. "To keep our stocks of food and fuel up, you have to squirm your way into these sorts of places. What am I supposed to do if something happens to you? I can't come in and get you, and then what? I'm supposed to starve? Or worse still, what happens when the storm pulls these places down for good? Or everything gets scavenged, or goes out of date?"

"Jesus, Jack, chill-."

"Stop telling me to chill out. You might be happy to wander this fucking wasteland, digging around in dangerous shitholes, but you need to think!"

"I am thinking!" Ada replied, forcefully tossing a bag into the van. "Look at that building, Jack. No. Actually look at it."

Jack rolled his eyes and turned around.

"This is our world now, right? We can't just pop to the shops to pick up our weekly shop because everywhere looks like this."

"What's your point?"

"My point is, we didn't ask for this, but bitching and moaning isn't going to solve anything. This is the hand we've been dealt, right? So we've got to make the best of it."

"By killing ourselves to rescue fucking sleeping bags!"

"To trade! Jesus, have you not heard a word I've been

saying?"

"There's no-one out here, Ade. And if there were, what's to say they're not in worse shape? You think they're just going to have an infinite supply of food to give away for this shit?"

"Of course I don't! But they might have *some* food, and if they're willing to give us some in exchange for a warm sleep, or a means to cook that food, then I'd make that deal. Besides, once people's minds are off the freezing at night problem, they might move on to solving the long-term food problem."

"I think you're delusional."

"Well, at least I'm doing something! I don't hear you coming up with any ideas!"

Ada slammed the side door shut and stomped through the mud to her vehicle; a Mercedes Unimog that was taller than the remains of the building it was parked beside.

"Are we going, or what?"

Jacked looked over with a frown. "Yeah. But where?"

"Seriously? I thought we were going back to that family manor of yours."

"Why?"

"Well, that driveway was pretty clear and out in the open. You know the location, it's a good base camp, you know?"

"If you ignore the crumbling mansion…" Jack straightened up, shaking his head. "We're not going back there."

"I…" Ada sighed, then nodded. "Alright. Well, using the same logic, I saw a golf course across the road?"

Jack shrugged. "Lead on."

Ten minutes later, after using a mix of metal fencing and trees to cross an overflowing trench, Ada and the Unimog pulled up on the driving range. Jack stopped his van several meters away and jumped out.

"Yeah?" Ada asked, joining him.

Jack nodded. "Yeah. Nice and open. We should be safe here."

"I might see if I can improve my swing too."

"Let's deal with dinner first, eh?"

"Sure thing, chef. What's on the menu?"

Jack shrugged. "You tell me?"

"Er, well… Chicken curry, cheesy pasta, chilli and rice-"

"Yeah, yeah, very funny."

Ada blinked. "I'm serious." She stepped over to the van and pulled the door open. She pulled one of the bags closer and unzipped it. "See?"

He took a packet out and studied it. "Pasta bolognese?"

"Just add boiling water," Ada replied with a grin. "Lucky dip!" She stuffed her hand in and pulled out another. "Hmm… All-day breakfast. Suits me."

"These are a bit of a step up from the MRE's I was on."

"I told you I was thinking."

Jack shook his head. "Maybe, in your own way. But that wasn't what I meant. Sure, you can find this stuff, but at enormous risk to yourself. I'm saying we need something else. Something safer, that both of us can do."

Ada opened her mouth to say something, got caught in a thought, then smiled. "I get it now. Feeling left out while I have all the fun?"

Jack grabbed a flat camping stove off the passenger seat and set it up at the side door. "Your idea of fun and mine are very different. But I suppose so, I'm a mechanic, used to getting my hands dirty, not standing about while someone else does all the heavy lifting."

"Well, we've already established you're not coming in with me. Besides, if something happens to you, we won't be able to keep the vehicles running. And if I get killed, I want you to take the Unimog. As impressive as your Transit is, Moggy clears roads."

"We're not talking about this now." Jack filled a metal teapot from a jerry can and set it down on the stove. "Let's assume both of us live for the foreseeable future, I need to be put to better use."

"Well… I dunno? The vehicles we've got are perfectly suited for what's going on… Although I suppose you could always repair the wrecks out here, trade them to other people?"

"Less reliance on these 'other people' please. In fact, our plans should be extremely selfish, to the point that if we split up, we don't need the other to survive, not because I plan on going anywhere, but because out here, anything could happen."

Ada nodded. "Yeah… you're right."

"So put that little genius brain of yours to work and think of something."

She grinned. "If I didn't know any better, I'd say that was a compliment."

"If you say so."

Ada tore the top off her meal and stepped over to the stove.

She set it down on the side and gingerly poured up to the line. Within seconds, the air around her filled with the aroma of a freshly cooked breakfast. "Oh damn."

"No kidding," Jack replied. "Smells great."

"Here, let's do yours."

Ada repeated the procedure, only spilling a little boiling water on the inner step.

"Eh." Jack shrugged. "I think yours smells better."

"Plenty to choose from for next time."

"Yeah… I suppose so…"

* * *

"Alright," Ada said, getting comfortable in the passenger seat with her trusty fork. "How about this, we get ourselves a couple of caravans, tear the roofs off those suckers, put some glass or perspex or whatever up there instead, then we've got ourselves a pair of rolling greenhouses."

Jack glanced over at her from the driver's seat. "Uhh, it's a little ambitious, don't you think?"

"Well, it's my first idea, so help me out."

"I didn't say it was bad," Jack replied, blowing his dinner and watching as the windows steamed up. "I just said it was ambitious."

Ada shrugged. "Ambitious? What's-"

"Well, firstly, we need to find two intact caravans out here, and since they're usually made out of weaker materials than cars and trucks, that isn't likely. Then we gotta find some transparent material, in a world where glass seems to be the first thing on the storm's hit list."

"Okay, so there's a couple of problems, but we can work it out."

"I uh…" Jack jabbed his fork into his food and rubbed his forehead. "I guess trailers would be more likely to survive."

Ada grinned. "Okay, you're problem-solving. Love it."

"Find a trailer, and you can build whatever you want on top. We'd have to find a welder and something to power it to make something really sturdy. Failing that, I think I can figure something out if we find a microwave."

Ada froze midway to her mouth with a forkful of steaming beans. "A… microwave?"

Jack nodded. "Yeah. I need the transformer. And a couple of batteries. And some very thick cable. I've got some welding rods in the van."

"I don't follow, but if you say you can do it, I believe you."

"Easy, we're just spitballing ideas here. It'd be better if we just found a welder and a generator, but microwaves and car batteries are more common."

"So we get the trailer and the welder, what next?"

"Well, we'd need metal. Again, not an issue considering the scrapheap that fills the roads nowadays. Then it's just a case of glass, or whatever, and the stuff you need to grow plants."

"For glass…" Ada replied. "Could we not just use the surviving windscreens?"

"I'm not sure. Windscreens are protected against UV, so what does that mean for the plants?"

"No clue, but it probably isn't good." Ada tapped her fork against her teeth, looking up at the sun-visor. "What about an office building?"

"Good luck finding one with an intact panel, and they're probably protected too."

"Damn it," Ada said, relaxing back again. "I wish I knew more about this stuff."

"How about tarp? Like transparent plastic sheeting?"

Ada grinned. "Now that sounds like something we can get our hands on."

"Just for the roof though, we don't want to advertise that we're carrying food-bearing plants."

"Sounds like we need to find a D.I.Y. store."

"We keep heading east, we'll find one."

"I've been meaning to ask, where are we going?"

"I don't know. Deeper into London. Maybe there are other survivors but at this point, I'm not holding my breath."

"Lots of tube stations to hide from the weather."

"Yeah, but can they cope with the amount of water the storm brings with it?"

"Hey, if we find people, we find people, if not, then we'll keep doing what we're doing, albeit this time with an eye to fixing up some trailers."

"It's going to take time for things to grow, and we might not be able to provide ourselves with everything we need from just the trailers."

"We'll aim for big trailers… Moggy can certainly handle it."

"Again, missing the point."

"Look, if it comes to it, we can hunt, right? Still birds out there. I think I saw a squirrel earlier."

Jack frowned, folded his empty packet, then set it on the dash with his fork on top. He reached into his pocket for his cigarettes, tossing the box into the cup holder between them.

Ada nodded. "Cheers."

"And how exactly do you plan on 'hunting' in a country with such strong firearms control? You can't just scavenge a rifle over here."

"Bows, slings, you know, like how people used to do it before guns." She rubbed her hands then reached for the cigarettes. "I saw a TV show once. They'd made a shotgun out of some scaffolding and a stapler."

"On TV?"

"Well, okay, they didn't *make* it on TV. It was a documentary on some prison and they were showing off all the weapons they'd collected over the years."

"A staple gun, and a bit of scaffolding?"

Ada waved her hand. "I'm sure it was a bit more in-depth than that, but mostly, yeah." She lit the cigarette before passing the lighter over and cracking the window a sliver. "I'm not suggesting we make one, no ammo, but still…"

"Right. Hunting. Should we gather berries too?"

Ada frowned. "I know you're being facetious, but scouring allotments for food isn't a bad idea."

"You know I was wrong about you. You're always thinking,

eh?"

"Told you."

They smoked in silence for a few moments. After a while, Jack glanced over to Ada. "They kept all the weapons they'd confiscated at the prison?"

"Yeah, why?"

"Uh, no reason. Just seems like a dumb idea is all."

* * *

"Heathrow airport, coming up." Jack's voice sounded distorted through the bright yellow walkie-talkie tacked to Ada's dash. She jabbed at the button. "You're supposed to say 'over', over."

"Why? We're not in the military."

"No, but we are truckers! Over."

"Roads blocked up ahead. Gonna pull it over here for a minute anyway."

"Good idea. We can scope it out! Over."

They pulled up short of an overturned bus. Ada turned the

engine off and jumped out.

"Gonna take two of us to move this I reckon."

"Later. I don't suppose you grabbed some binoculars yesterday?"

Ada nodded. "In one of the black bags."

"I'll go find them. See if you can find a way onto that bus."

"Onto it as in inside it, or onto it as in on top?"

"On top. I want to see what's happened here."

Ada raised her hand to the chaos beyond the many fences.

"Uh, I'll save you the time; a bunch of planes have smashed into one another and are lying in bits across the runways and in the terminal buildings." She frowned. "Surprised to see the control tower still mostly intact though."

"How it avoided the rest of this destruction is puzzling. Maybe we can use that."

Ada sighed. "Alright then. Go find stuff, I'll be climbing around this thing."

She cautiously wandered around the large pool of oil and fuel that surrounded the bus until she came to the front. Ada tilted her head to the side in an attempt to read the info-bar but quickly realised that the display had glitched.

"Eh… probably just airport transport…" She straightened up and continued on.

Reaching the other side, the true extent of the damage became clear. The roof had buckled, tiny chunks of glass floated on the puddle of oil, and the frame had twisted beyond recognition. As Ada got closer, a now familiar smell crept into her nostrils. Reaching into her pockets, she pulled out a pouch and folded it into her scarf before wrapping it around her face. She inhaled, then sighed, the smell had already gotten in, and no amount of flowers or perfume would change that.

She slipped her hands into a pair of tight gloves, then pulled herself up onto the remains of the rooftop ventilation system. With a firm foothold, Ada looked over the edge. Peering inside through a broken window she could see several shadowy masses lying on the ground below her inside the bus. Ada shivered, gulped, then focused and pulled herself farther up.

"How's it look?" Jack asked.

"Like it did on the ground, just from higher up!"

"Very funny." He glanced around, then back up at Ada as she carefully navigated the top of the wrecked vehicle. "How'd you get up there?"

"Some kind of air conditioning system on the roof. Be careful, there's not a lot of places to walk up here."

After some grunting and cursing, Jack eventually joined Ada and handed her a pair of binoculars.

"Er, what are we looking for?"

He shrugged, then raised a pair to his own eyes. "Just thought you'd wanna have a look too."

"Oh, yes, the broken planes vista looks wonderful this time of day. I'm particularly fond of the bold new shapes of terminal three. Do you think the wing sticking out the roof cost them much to do?"

"Don't be such a smart-ass. Besides, there isn't much roof left…"

"Look, if we're gonna raid this place, let's just get it over and done with already."

Jack lowered his binoculars and glanced at her. "You seem spooked."

"Yeah, maybe I am. Standing on a bus full of bodies while we look out over an abandoned airport has that effect on me."

"Ah! And the reality of the situation finally hits her."

"What?"

"You're fine with this whole apocalypse thing until you're forced to confront the human cost." He lifted the binoculars to his eyes again. "This isn't a game. People, probably *good* people, were caught up in all this too."

"Probably some bad ones too. But you already know how I feel about that. This 'storm', it's a punishment, right? Mother nature giving humanity the boot because we ruined the planet."

"Looking at this, I'd say she did a better job than we ever could…"

"Oh what? A bit of torn up tarmac and some smashed planes? Give it a couple of years, this place will be full of wildlife, trees, plants, you name it. Remember Chernobyl?"

"If humanity had been given more time, we might have come up with a solution."

"Yeah, well we'll never know now will we?" Ada sighed. "Look, are we raiding this place or not?"

"You see down there? By the hanger?"

Ada raised her binoculars. "What am I looking for?"

"That white one rolled into the doorframe. I'm pretty sure that's a generator."

"The trailer thing?"

"That's the one. Airport vehicles aren't really in my wheelhouse though."

"And we can use that to power a welder if we find one?"

"And a whole bunch of other stuff too."

"Well, you can go nuts. I'm heading to the terminal building to loot the food."

Jack glanced over at her. "You're not gonna help?"

Ada scoffed. "Help? What help can I provide? You roll it back over with the Transit, then get to work on it with your magic engineer hands." She started towards the edge and lowered herself down. "Besides, we need food more than we need electricity."

"The electricity is a part of the long-term food plan."

"Yeah, I know that, so while you're dealing with the long-term, I'm looking out for the short-term."

"Alright, fine. Stay in touch on the radio."

"Walkie-talkies!" Ada corrected as she wandered back to the Unimog.

"And be careful!"

Jack looked through the binoculars again as the roar of Ada's engine filled the air. He heard it revving loudly, then jerked his head around just in time to see her crashing through the metal fence surrounding the airport. The Unimog flattened any resistance before rolling over it.

In her side mirror, Ada could see Jack standing there on the bus, open-mouthed, arms down by his sides as if ready to give up. She offered him an unseeable grin, then tore off down the ruined runway towards the terminal building.

"You didn't have to do that you know?"

Ada slipped her earphones into the walkie-talkie and hit the button. "You wanna move a bus full of bodies, that's on you. Also, you're welcome? Over."

"For what?"

"For making an opening? Over."

"Oh yeah, fantastic. How many spare tyres do you think I've got?"

"Jesus, Jack, stop whining. If you want to go through security, check in your luggage and wait for your flight, go ahead!" She paused, then added. "Over."

"Stop saying that! We're not truckers and we're not in the military!"

Ada reached over and turned the dial down. "Oh? What's

that? Sorry, can't hear you, going into a tunnel, bye."

"You're on a run-"

The light faded and Ada blew the air out of her cheeks.

"Jesus… What a whiny bitch!" She adopted a mocking voice. "Hey *'Ade'*, please stop getting us into places and retrieving food because really you should be thinking long-term. Oh, what's that? You're thinking long-term? You're neglecting our short-term." She smacked the steering wheel. "Give me a break, man!"

She drove between, under and around several big plane parts. Wings, noses, landing equipment, tails. Ada wasn't paying attention other than to what she needed to avoid.

"Oh, hey *'Ade'*, why don't we stop at this creepy fucking airport instead of getting to London and finding more people. *Alright, fine Jack, let's stop at the creepy airport.* Oh hey *'Ade'*, where you going? *To get food.* Well, *'Ade'*, make sure you respect the perimeter fence, we wouldn't want to cause, any, fucking, damage, now, would, we?! *God! What a clueless asshole!*"

The Unimog rumbled to a stop beside a massive opening revealing three levels of crumbling floors beyond it. Ada switched off the engine, pocketed the key and the walkie-talkie, then jumped down to the cracked pavement below. Shutting the door, she took a deep breath.

"Alright, Ada, just chill out. You haven't got to deal with his shit, for now, so let's just take it easy and get it done."

She tightened her scarf, then strapped on her goggles before pressing through the gap. The terminal building was huge, but any sense of distance was obscured by the collapsed upper levels and the mess of plane components scattered throughout. Ada could hear the roof creaking in the wind, and the scratching of metal against broken glass.

Zipping up her coat, Ada moved quickly through the check-in area and up the dead escalators into a security area. Her nostrils flared under the scarf as the familiar smell rolled over her. It was stronger this time and came with a coppery shadow. As she passed through the scanner, Ada froze in her tracks. Ahead of her, two bodies lay in a pool of claret. A bloody trail led away from them, into the shopping section. She followed the trail with her eyes before it disappeared out of view.

"Right," Ada said to herself. "You knew it would come to this.

Now you've got two options; turn around and walk back to the truck, or stay here, loot the shit out of this place, but potentially have to deal with violent survivors in the process." She patted herself down. "Inventory is limited. Need a weapon if we go that route." She glanced back to the escalators. "They can't steal Moggy, they need my key, and all of the good loot is with Jack… This would only be a risk to myself, and it looks as though my potential enemy could be wounded. So how do I do this?"

Ada quietly approached the bodies. She didn't look at them long before turning away and heading towards the security office. There were several scratch marks around the lock, and a trail of scuff marks leading from it towards the violent scene. Ada closed her eyes as her mind tried piecing it all together.

Two shadows reach the top of the elevator and move quickly towards the shopping area. The door to the security room flies open and out runs a third shadow towards them. The three meet, there's a struggle, then one of the shadows pulls himself away, leaving the other two bleeding out on the floor.

Ada opened her eyes again and immediately reached out for the wall. She took a deep breath to steady herself and clear away the dizziness. "Jesus... that was weird."

After gathering her bearings, Ada wrapped her hand around the handle and pulled down. The lock gave way without protest. She quickly pushed through into the room beyond. After briefly scanning around and discovering herself alone, Ada pressed her head to the door crack and peeked out, wondering if anyone had heard her.

"Where the hell is everyone...? We can't be the only survivors. And surely those that are left should be helping one another... Not beating each other to death..."

Once she was happy that the coast was clear, she pulled out her wind-up torch and gave it a few spins. It whined quietly, but in the near-silence of the airport, Ada thought it sounded deafening.

She flicked the switch and swept her surroundings with the dull beam of warm light. The floor was covered in sheets of paper, open filing cabinets lined the far wall next to a door with a card reader. Turning to her right, she saw three dead monitors sitting atop a desk. Shining her light between them, Ada saw a couple of thick black vests.

"Jackpot." She said as she approached. Setting the flashlight down, Ada squirmed out of her coat and tossed it over the lone chair before picking up one of the vests. "Damn... well, they ain't light, that's for sure." It was covered in pockets and had the word 'Security' velcroed to the back. Tapping at one of the pouches gave Ada a sore knuckle. "Ow. Ha. No way. Bulletproof Ada!"

She pulled it over her head and stepped back, trying to get a feel for the additional weight. Despite being nearly the right size for her, it still felt loose. After almost a minute of pulling straps and yanking at velcro strips, it eventually sat comfortably on her shoulders, and tight around her chest and stomach.

She gave the room another cursory glance, slipped back into her coat, straightened out her scarf and goggles, then peered through the crack in the door once more. Things still looked very much as she had left them. Not sensing any threats, and feeling bolder now she was wearing some protection, Ada stepped back out into the security area.

She made her way over to the bodies again, then began following the trail. Her eyes darted around as she reached the shopping area. One of the duty-free adverts had a bloody handprint on the surround, the sight of it slowed her to a more cautious speed and encouraged her to find some means of self-defense.

"This place has held up really well…" She whispered to herself as she moved toward a juice stand. "I should tell Jack… Might be we can settle here for a spell… Ah, damn it." Reaching into her pocket, she flicked the walkie-talkie back on and pressed the button.

"Hey, Jack, can you hear me? Over."

After a few seconds, her earphones crackled to life. "Where the hell have you been?"

"Er, in the terminal building, as I said. Over."

"I meant on the radio. I've been trying to get in touch for ages."

"Why, what's up? Over."

"It's not a generator. Well, it has one, but I think they used it for supplying power to parked aircraft."

"Can we use it? Over."

"Parts of it. There's some good stuff here. I'm going to hitch it up to the Transit and come join you."

"Be careful. I think there's someone else in here with me. I've come across two bodies, badly beaten, but evidence suggests a third person got away. Over."

There was a brief moment of silence, then Jack asked.

"Bodies?"

"Yeah, and not victims of the storm either. Well… I suppose they were in a way, but either I'm about to find a third body, someone who is willing to kill, or someone who was just trying to defend themselves. And to be honest, I ain't having much luck finding anything to defend myself with. Over."

"Get out of there, Ade. You could be in serious trouble."

She overturned a box of cutlery and began looking through the contents.

"What? No way! There could be another survivor here! And from the looks of it, they're in bad shape already. Goddamnit, why is everything in this fucking airport made of plastic!"

"Do you really need to ask? And what if they're not alone?"

"Uh. Look, I need a way to defend myself. Any ideas? Over."

"This is a bad idea, Ade."

"I know the risks, Jack. Weapons, now. Over."

"Alright, fine. Don't say I didn't warn you. What about… hmm… they sell deodorant, right?"

Ada's eyes shot up and focussed on the Perfume shop opposite. "Hold that thought, over."

"While you're there, try finding a lighter too, they sometimes give them away with boxes of cigarettes, but if not, duty-free shops should have lighters for sale."

"The shutter is down. I can't see a way in. Over."

"Damn. Okay, what *is* open? What have we got to work with?"

"Uhh…" Ada turned and scanned the still open stores. Her choices were limited. "W H Jones, uh, a coffee shop, one of the gambling areas, a suitcase shop, and Whisky World. Over."

"They sell glass bottles in Whisky World?"

"Let's find out."

Ada was out of breath by the time she'd reached the entrance.

"Made it…" She wheezed. "Damn it, I'm in bad shape."

"Ade? What's wrong? Are you okay?"

"Yeah. Yeah. I found a bullet-proof vest in the security office. Thing's heavy as hell. Over."

"You found armour, but no weapons?"

"There was a keycard door. They probably don't keep them handy. Over." She pulled a bottle of extremely dark brown fluid off the shelf, then glanced at the price tag. "Holy shit. Hey, Jack, what does cheap whiskey look like? Over."

"I dunno? Why does it matter?"

"Well, I'm keeping this for myself. Think it'd be better to smash a bottle in the sub-five-hundred quid range instead. Over." She put it on the counter with a smile. "I'll be back for you later."

"Well, the longer it's in the barrel, the darker it gets, so look for light stuff I guess?"

Beside the counter sat the bottom half of a barrel, inside which, several bottles rested upon neatly placed bundles of dead hay.

"Sixty quid. That's more like it." Without giving it a second thought, Ada grabbed the neck of the bottle and bashed it against the counter. The sound of smashing glass echoed across the terminal. when Ada opened her eyes again, her glove was soaked through, and barely any of the bottle remained.

"Damn." She said, pressing the button with her other hand.

"They make that look easy in the films."

"What?"

"Breaking bottles. Over."

"Break two against each other, then use the best one."

"Eh, good thinking. Over."

"Hope you're wearing your goggles…"

After another deafening shattering, Ada looked down at the resultant mess. Tossing aside one, and reaching for the radio, Ada triumphantly exclaimed; "Got one! Over." before stepping out of the puddle of strong-smelling liquid around her.

"Good. Let's hope you don't have to use it."

"Rather have it and not need it than need it and not have it." She looked out to the concourse again. "Eh… you'd have thought all that noise would have attracted some attention. Over."

"You can't rely on them not knowing you're there. Just wait, I won't be long."

"Two possibilities, right? Either they're too wounded to fight, or they're waiting to ambush me. Over."

"Or they're dead."

"Or getting there. Feel like we've already wasted enough time. Over."

"Ade, I know you're a grown woman who can make her own decisions, but this could be life or death."

Leaving Whiskey World behind, Ada rediscovered the trail of blood and followed it towards W H Jones. Hiding behind a pillar near the entrance, Ada lowered her scarf slightly and peeled out an earphone. She couldn't hear anything but the groaning roof and the whistle of the wind. Creeping closer to the entrance, a firm grip on her makeshift weapon, she saw the trail leading through the main aisle to the rear of the shop. Ada took a deep breath, rubbed the plating in her vest, then slowly stepped forward, taking care to avoid the trail of bright red drops and footprints.

Crouching down at the display near the end of the aisle, Ada readied her bottle and leaned out.

"Oh. Fuck."

Ahead of her lay another body, he had a knife sticking upwards out of his chest, and was surrounded by a growing puddle of blood. A couple of torn open first aid packets littered the floor around him.

Ada stepped closer, noticing the smear mark running down the display he'd been propped up against. Then she heard a sound like a short, sharp gasp. The body flinched slightly causing Ada to jump.

"Jesus! You're still alive?"

His eyelids barely opened to reveal a set of hollow eyes that didn't so much stare at her as through her. Ada shivered as her blood ran cold. She took another deep breath, then knelt down, putting the bottle down behind her. "Jesus. Okay. Shit. I'm gonna be real honest with you here." She said, examining the damage. "All of my medical knowledge comes from TV shows, right?"

If he heard her, he didn't show it.

"From the looks of it, you've got a piercing wound to your chest, and this knife is the only thing stopping you from having a hole in your lung, but I don't think we should leave it in there…"

She looked up at his face again, blood ran from his mouth, his eyes swelled with bruising, and his lips quivered as he fought for air.

"Holy shit," Jack said as he turned the corner, gasping.

"He's still alive!" Ada replied. "But he won't be for much longer if we don't do something. I need you to find me a credit card, or a gift card or something similar, and some tape."

"You a medic or something?"

"I guess we're about to find out. Go on, go!"

As Jack disappeared over to the counter, Ada leaned down and whispered. "We're going to pull the knife out, okay? Now there's a good chance this will leave you with a sucking chest wound, which I'll need to fix by sealing the hole, right?"

His eyelids lazily flickered, then closed.

"Okay buddy, stay with me now. Jack! Where're those supplies?"

"Right here." He dropped down by her side and spread several gift cards and a roll of packing tape out on the floor.

"Alright, good." She picked up one of the cleaner med-kits and found a pair of gloves. "See if you can find yourself a pair, I'm going to need your help."

He obeyed automatically, reaching up for a new packet off the shelf.

"Okay." Ada blew the air out of her cheeks and looked down. "I'm going to take the knife out, I need you to roll his shirt up and apply pressure to the wound, okay?"

"Apply- With my hands?"

"Yeah. The gloves should be clean, and it's only for a few seconds." She grabbed one of the gift cards and set it down on her knee. Next, she took the roll of tape and ripped off several strips before attaching them around three edges of the plastic square.

"Where did you learn this?"

"Er..." Ada said, flipping it over so it was sticky side up. "I read about it in a newspaper. A soldier helped someone in a bar fight by doing this."

She unwrapped a sterile wipe and looked over at Jack with focused eyes. "Are you ready?"

He frowned. "Fuck no, I ain't ready. But there isn't much choice, is there?"

"No. Now, remember, I pull it out, you pull his shirt up, apply pressure."

After another deep breath, Ada reached out and wrapped her hands around the handle. She bit her lip, and despite some fluid noises, pulled the intruding blade straight up and out. Jack reached out and grabbed the hole in his shirt and ripped it open before pressing both hands against his chest.

Ada pulled out the sterile wipe. "Right, stage two, cleaning it up quickly. When I say, I need you to lift your hands up, let me clean it, then apply pressure again, okay?"

"Just get on with it."

"Okay, hands up."

Ada hastily wiped away as much blood as she dare. As soon as she pulled the blood-soaked wipe away, Jack placed his hands back down again.

"Okay, last part now." She nodded to the barely conscious victim. "Can you hear his breathing?"

Jack tilted his head, then nodded. "It's weak, but I can hear it."

"Okay cool. When he exhales, get your hands clear, okay?"

"Alright…" He got a little closer, then started breathing in time. "It's a little irregular but…" He inhaled, then sharply exhaled, then inhaled again. Just as he was breathing out, Jack lifted his hands clear out the way, and Ada slapped the gift card in place over the wound, careful to seal up all but one of the edges.

"Why only three sides?"

Ada shrugged. "This is what I read. I think the card acts as a valve or something. Let's air out, but not in?"

"And the bleeding?"

"I'm going to use a gauze and some of this bandage to keep pressure on it, but I can't mess up that gift-card deal."

Jack took hold of the gauze and nodded. "I've got this."

"Ah yeah, right, valves. Engineering. I get it."

"And your hands are starting to shake. Go on, take five."

Jack carefully went to work as Ada got to her feet,

There was a gasp of air, then another. Ada glanced over at him, then down at Jack. "I think… We did it?"

"You didn't learn that from a newspaper."

"You're right," Ada replied. "But it sounds better than 'I saw it on a Webflix show once'."

"Does it?"

Ada waved her hands, then pulled the bloody gloves off. "If this works, then it doesn't matter does it?"

"And what are we supposed to do with him now? What if he's the one who attacked those other people?"

"Eh. He's in no state to hurt anyone now if that's the case…" She looked down at him, raising her voice. "But if he moves about too much, he could hurt himself beyond our meager skills."

Looking around, she spotted a display near the counter and wandered over. "Also, a blanket. Don't want him to survive a stabbing just to die from hypothermia or shock."

"You sure you don't have any medical training?"

"None. Although I got over my fear of needles by watching

House, guess some stuff just stuck."

"Yeah, well I wouldn't go banking on T.V. knowledge for everything."

She stepped back over, pulling the tag off a couple of blankets. "Here." She passed them over to Jack, then opened another packet and began inflating a neck pillow.

Once he looked as comfortable as a stabbing victim could given the circumstances, Ada and Jack wandered out of earshot.

"So, what now?"

Ada shrugged. "I was gonna fill a bunch of suitcases and load the Moggy up, but someone is going to have to stay with him."

"Why? You already saved his life, isn't that enough?"

Ada shook her head. "I'm not leaving him. He's still going to need our help, I mean, his recovery is going to take a while."

"So what? We just hang out at this airport waiting for more trouble to turn up?"

"No… I mean, the airport is in pretty good shape, but you're right…" She sighed. "We hang around here, it's likely we're going to need more gift cards."

"What a fucking mess…" Jack said, more to himself than

anyone else.

"Yeah, I know it's bad. But look at it this way, we found another survivor, right?"

"One who might have killed two other people!"

"And if that's the case then we'll deal with it. Right now, we can't even ask him any questions, so one thing at a time."

"I swear, Ade, this is gonna be trouble."

"You can't know that. Now look, we've got two problems. Firstly, we can't leave him there, so one of us is going to have to find a stretcher or something we can use to move him with. Secondly, we need to loot this place, getting as much stuff as we can before getting out of here. Have you got room in the Transit?"

"I can tidy it up."

"Good, because we're gonna be turning it into an ambulance."

Jack blinked. "You want *me* to look after him?"

"No, I want to put him in your vehicle. We use the Moggy to clear routes, right? That's not as smooth a ride as any vehicle that follows behind. If he starts freaking out or whatever, call me on the radio and I'll stop and come to check on him. Hell, I'll even sleep in your rig if it makes you feel better."

"Alright. And what about the Unimog?"

"Easy, we fill it to the brim with all the stuff we take from here."

Jack nodded. "Looks like there's enough food in here to keep us stocked for a while."

"Don't forget all that booze too. Drink is a good tr-" She paused. "Let's just take what we can."

"We don't need to stay by this guys side, do we? I mean we could both go fill some cases, then check on him every now and then."

Ada nodded. "I guess you're right."

"And, I think we should pile everything up here first, then take it all down to the vans in as few a trips as possible."

She shrugged. "Anything that speeds up our time in here is fine by me."

"Alright, then, in that case, let's get to it." He turned, then paused and reached for his back pocket. "Oh yeah, what do you want me to do with this?" He pulled out the knife with a frown.

"Probably best you keep hold of it for now. Knives are useful."

"I'll try to turn it away from its life of crime."

Ada grinned. "Glad to hear it." She motioned to the other shops. "Come on, we've got work to do."

The following hour went by in a blur. First, they helped themselves to the largest suitcases they could find. Then, Jack disappeared into the coffee shop. Ada was too busy pilfering any meals-to-go that were still in date to see him emerge lugging two unwieldy cases of his own. After dropping them off in the security area, away from the bodies, he joined Ada with a couple more and started filling them with crisps, sweets, and drinks.

"Getting the important stuff, eh?" Ada asked.

"Seems like you've got that covered, but some extra sugar won't hurt."

"Eh, fair enough."

He lifted a bottle of blue liquid off the dead refrigerator shelf and glanced at the label. "These ones with electrolytes are especially good."

"Ah yeah," Ada replied. "Any drink that's the same colour as toilet cleaner has got to be good for you, right?"

Jack laughed. "Blueberries are pretty healthy and they're blue."

"Yeah, okay, I'll give you that one."

"How's our friend?"

"Sleeping. Breathing."

"I can't believe you knew how to do all that."

"Yeah, well we'll see how it holds up. Speaking of which, are there any medical books in here?"

"I should think so. I'll go check."

He finished emptying the shelves, then headed for the section near the back full of reading material.

"Might be an idea to grab a bunch of stuff," Ada called over.

"Anything in non-fiction."

"Alright."

They continued their looting spree until the light from outside began to fade.

"Hey, Ade, we should get moving."

"Sure thing." She replied, stepping around the massive pile of cases while trying to put a stretcher together as she carried a case under her arm.

"Where the hell did you find that?" Jack asked.

"Staff only section. I was looking for the toilet. Oh, and here." She tossed over a green med-box with a white cross on the front. "A proper kit, not like those tourist versions."

"Alright, good find."

"Here, help me with this."

She handed the stretcher over to Jack then started towards W H Jones with him following behind.

"I can't believe we're taking him with us."

"Afraid so" Ada replied. "Look, if you want, we can secure him to that thing, but I really don't think he's a threat. I reckon he got ambushed while exploring this place and barely survived."

"Securing him might not be a bad idea. We don't need him waking up and re-opening something."

"Okay, good thinking," Ada replied. "Now, before we go, are we sure we got everything?"

"We've emptied the shelves in here, the stockroom in the coffee shop, Whisky World is more like Whisky City now, I've got all the cigarettes and painkillers left in here." He nodded. "Yeah, I think we're good."

"Okay, how do you want to do this?"

"I reckon we should take him to the Transit first, then one of us brings the luggage downstairs, while the other loads it into the Moggy."

"There was another vest in the security office. Looked small, but maybe you can use it." She bit her lip. "You know. Just in case."

Jack nodded. "I won't say no to bullet-proof armour."

"Okay, well…" Ada motioned to their barely conscious friend.

"Let's get this over with."

Ada cleared away enough empty packaging and med-kits for Jack to put the stretcher down.

"You take his legs," Jack said, moving into position near his head.

"We need to do this quickly, but carefully."

"I know, I know." He knelt down, then looked over at Ada. "On three?"

She nodded, taking hold of his legs.

"One. Two. Three!"

With strained grunting, they managed to lift him onto the stretcher, seemingly without doing any further damage.

"Is he okay?" Jack asked.

"No. But he's still breathing, so that's a plus."

"Come on, let's get him downstairs before the night really hits."

The two of them managed to lift the stretcher and started towards the security area.

"What about the runway?" Ada asked.

"For our overnight stay?"

"We'll park far enough away from anything that might fall on us." Ada paused, then knelt down. "Hold on, hold on. Between him and this vest, I'm running out of steam here."

"Alright, take five." His eyes fell on the security office. "Besides, this'd be a good time to get a vest of my own."

"They're on the desk. Should be two left."

"I'll grab both. No telling when we might need them."

After disappearing for several seconds, Jack reemerged into the security hall with a grin. "You were right about them being small, but I think I can make this work. You ready to get going?"

"Yeah, yeah. Come on, let's do this."

By the time they made it out to the Unimog, the sun was already dipping below the horizon. They slowly trudged over to the Transit and put the stretcher on the kerb. Jack then hopped up into his van and started a very brisk clean-up, making sure everything was secured in place with straps and rope, but leaving enough space for the stretcher, and somewhere to sleep.

"Won't be able to walk through from the 'cab'," Jack said, jumping back down. "But that's as much space as I can offer without stuff rolling all over the place."

"Looks good to me. We lay him down on these bags here?" She motioned to the pile on the right looking in through the back doors.

"Yeah. We'll keep him on the stretcher and wrap him up with some more blankets, the insulation in here isn't great."

"Oh! Maybe we could use some of those sleeping bags you said were a waste of time!"

Without saying another word, Jack wandered over to their patient and motioned for Ada to help him. They lifted the stretcher onto the pile of bags, then Jack moved around to help Ada push him in. After strapping him down with some bungee cords, careful to avoid his chest, they stepped back and sighed with relief.

"Alright, now for those suitcases."

Ada nodded. "I'll go back up and bring them down. You run them to the Unimog. Just stick em where ever they'll fit. And any time you get a free second, come to check on our friend here, make sure moving him hasn't messed anything up."

She jogged back over to her vehicle, hopped up on the rear step, fiddled with her key for a spell, then popped the back door open. There was barely enough light to illuminate the single cloth-covered mattress, a small pile of toilet paper, and the few cardboard boxes full of food that barely made a dent in the massive space. She flipped the mattress up against the side, stacked the boxes on the pallets underneath, then hopped back down giving Jack a thumbs up.

It took several trips across, up, down, and around before Ada was tugging the last of the cases down the escalator.
"Should really… have ditched… this armour… Holy shit."
She wheeled them across the check-in area to the hole in the wall. Jack took hold and carried them the final few meters to the Unimog.
"That's all of them," Ada said proudly.
"All this stuff reduces the usefulness of our vehicles. You can't sleep in here now."
"Maybe not, but we've got alternatives, right? Besides, I'd rather have this stuff and have to sleep in the Transit, than not have it."
"Oh, would you now?" Jack replied, grinning. "This morning I

didn't have any 'roommates' now I've got two."

"Yeah, I get it, it's not ideal…"

"Hopefully, only temporary too." He motioned toward the runway. "We should park up for the night, I'm starving."

Ada frowned. "Didn't you snack while we were up there?"

"My body doesn't run on sweets," Jack replied, turning to his van. "We should try to park up somewhere we can't be seen easily. You know, use the terminal buildings and hangers to cover ourselves."

"Hey!" Ada called after him. "What's the problem? We expecting visitors?"

He turned back, shaking his head. "No, but I don't want to meet the same fate as our friend here. This place looks tempting as hell, we should be prepared."

She exhaled, then nodded. "Yeah… okay, good thinking. I'll follow you."

As Ada settled into the driver's seat, she yawned, then rubbed her face in an attempt to shake off the tiredness. Turning the key, the Unimog rumbled to life. A lazy grin briefly swept across her face. Ada rolled the window down, took a deep breath, then put foot to pedal. As she turned, she could feel the extra resistance in the steering wheel from the additional weight.

Jack drove carefully, occasionally slowing to inspect the ruins of a hangar or some overturned boarding stairs before moving on. They wound through the airplane graveyard and around an old storage shed that had dumped its torn and twisted roof on the tarmac before pulling off the runway into the remains of a loading area. Jacked slowed once more to examine the circle of rubble surrounding them before coming to a stop at a clear patch near the center.
Ada rolled to a stop several meters away, ensuring she kept a large enough gap between the two vehicles.

* * *

"So…" Ada started, sat on the power-unit tow bar, poking at her steaming meal packet with a fork. "What's our next move?"
"Not sure," Jack replied, sitting down beside her. "And while It's great that we got all this stuff, we can't drive about with it all…"

"We haven't exactly got anywhere to put it…"

"Maybe not. But perhaps we can find somewhere."

"Like where? With that storm still hanging around, and the potential for more earthquakes, we won't be building anything for a while. And it's not like we can just take one that's still standing, chances are, it won't stay that way."

Jack nodded. "I'm surprised this airport has survived as well as it has. But you're right, even that terminal building will fall next time the storm hits it."

"So what are we supposed to do?"

"Not sure. What I do know is that all that extra weight is going to kill our fuel."

"Ah," Ada replied. "I hadn't thought of that."

"We need to think about our priorities. Why are we going to London?"

"You know why, we're looking for more survivors."

Jack shook his head. "Not anymore." He glanced over at their patient through the open rear doors. "After seeing what people are doing to each other, we need to avoid contact with anyone we find until we know what their intentions are."

Ada sighed. "How's he doing?"

"As good as can be expected I suppose. But don't change the

subject, we need a better plan."

"Ugh. I don't know, Jack. This is just one isolated incident, isn't it?"

"How can we know?"

"I guess… we can't." Ada sighed. "Okay, you've made your point. But if we're not going deeper into London, then where?"

"Maybe we should think about heading out to sea? I'm no expert, but I doubt earthquakes will have much effect on a boat."

"And risk getting caught up in the storm out there? No way." Ada jabbed her fork into her meal and let it sit there. "What about that place you came from? The… er… auxiliary place."

"It's smaller than my van, probably flooded by now too."

"But you said there were more, right?"

Jack nodded. "Yeah, but they'll be difficult to find, and we won't be able to store half this stuff in one."

"But there had to be bigger versions right? Like those doomsday bunkers, you always hear rich Americans buying."

Jack nodded. "I guess there'd be a few in the U.K? But again, how are we supposed to find something like that?"

"Eh… Maybe we don't have to find one?"

"What do you mean? You think we should build one?"

Ada nodded. "Why not? I mean, how hard could it be? We dig a hole, reinforce the hell out of it with… I dunno, wrecked plane parts? Weld it all together, then bury it again."

Jack looked at her with wide, questioning eyes. "You cannot be serious."

"It's better than your 'get lost at sea' idea!"

"You can't just 'build' something like that. You've got to think about drainage, ventilation, waste, how to get in and out, what happens if there's a fire, or-"

"Okay! Jack! Jesus wept."

"Also, you're moving the goalposts again. What happened to finding a trailer and making the rolling gardens?"

"Nuh-uh," Ada said, standing up and pointing her fork towards Jack. "You're not doing this again. Not now."

"Not doing what? And get that out of my face."

"Two minutes ago, you said 'We can't keep driving about.' Now you're saying we should be focusing on the trailers again, which means driving about. You're saying we can't build somewhere underground, but you're happy to go looking for some boat to throw yourself into the storm with. You say we need to avoid survivors, but you know as well as I do that whatever we plan on doing, we can't do it alone." She tossed the empty packet to one side and stepped back. "If anyone is changing the goalposts, it's you. Every time I come up with some plan or idea, you either agree to it until something better comes along or shoot it down straight away."

"I don't-"

"Yes, you do. Whenever I focus on our short-term survival, you give me shit for not paying attention to our long-term. And the reverse is also true. Look at the haul we got today, you've got some out of hand generator thing, and between us, we've got enough food to last us months. But instead of just celebrating that fact, you've got to be all 'well you forgot about this.' It's bullshit and it's driving me nuts."

"Celebrate?" Jack jumped to his feet. "I'm driving about, looting ruins in a world that could kill me with some weather. There is nothing to celebrate!"

As Ada drew breath to reply, she heard a groaning coming from the Transit. Glancing over, she saw their new friend moving slightly. Hopping up and kneeling by his side, Ada whispered. "Hey, it's okay. You're safe now."

"Uhh?"

"I need you to listen to me very carefully, okay?"

He blinked.

"Okay, that's good. Now, you need to try and remain as still as possible. What I'm about to tell you might come as a shock, but please don't move." She inhaled and let him digest her words for a few seconds. "Earlier today, you were in a fight of some kind. You sustained a serious chest wound that I and my... 'friend', patched up. I'm not a nurse or a doctor or whatever, neither is he, but you seem to be recovering. Now, I understand that you're probably thirsty, and a little hungry, but for reasons I can't explain, you can't eat or drink anything for a little while."

"C-Chrisss."

"Easy now. Is that your name?"

He moved his eyes from left to right slowly.

"Is Chris the person you were with at the airport?"

Another 'no' response from his eyes.

"Is Chris a different friend?"

This time, a gentle nod.

"Okay, that's good. Did Chris survive the storm?"

Another nod.

"And you want to find Chris?"

"Yesss. Can help... me..."

Ada glanced over at Jack. "He wants us to find someone."

"Well does he know where they are?"

"Gate... Gateway."

"Gateway?"

"Hm..." Jack replied. "Got anything else?"

"Wait. Gateway? Like, London Gateway? That massive port?"

"Yesss..."

"If we get you to London Gateway, there's help for you there?"

Ada looked back over at Jack. "They might have doctors or medics. We should get him there."

"He's a long way from L.G. Ask him how he got here."

He wheezed. "Underground..."

"You got a train?"

He closed his eyes, then opened them again slowly.

"Walked... Some..."

"You walked?" Ada frowned. "I guess the underground would be clearer than the roads..."

Jack nodded. "Yeah. Shame we can't use them."

"So what's the plan?"

"Well, I suppose we haven't got much choice, have we?"

"This could be good, Jack. It sounds like there are other survivors, and if they find out we rescued one of theirs-"

"Or they could mistake us for the people who did this to him and figure on repaying the favour."

Another wheeze. "You… welcome… Safe"

"Come on now, take it easy."

"What did he say?"

"He said we'd be welcomed. That it's safe."

"Anyone with a truck full of food and booze would be welcome anywhere. And if it's so safe, why's he out here with a hole in his chest?"

"So what's the alternative, Jack? What path are we going to follow until you change your mind?"

"Now hang on a min-"

"No, Jack. This man needs help, help that we can't provide. But we can get him somewhere that has that help. I can't do it alone, you know that, so let's just skip the bullshit argument and get straight to the doing." She got to her feet. "And, if this turns out to be a terrible idea, you can say 'I told you so'."

"If I still can."

Ada dropped down to the cement and fixed Jack with a stare. "You know how to get there?"

"London Gateway? Well… Yeah, follow the M-twenty-five around to the A-thirteen."

"Best you lock up then," Ada replied, storming over to her van. "We're going for a night drive."

Jack stood open-armed. "Seriously? After the day we've had you wanna go-" He waved his hands. "You know what? Fine. Whatever you say."

* * *

The Unimogs headlights shone brightly against flipped vehicles and loose trees before brushing them aside with little more than some loud revving and the grinding of metal on metal.

"You're going to be doing this all night."

Ada jabbed the walkie-talkie. "If that's the difference between him living in his friend's arms or dying in ours, I can go without the sleep. Over."

"Alright. But take it a bit easier will ya? I don't think this is what Mercedes had in mind."

"Our fuel situation," Ada replied, ignoring the question. "Could we empty some of these vehicles? Over."

"I haven't tried. Had enough fuel when I left the aux'. It's possible, could do it quickly if I had a fuel pump, some tubing, and a battery."

"Do you think we can make it to London Gateway before we run out? Over."

"Probably not. Besides, there's no guarantee whoever we're meeting will have fuel."

"How long will it take you to rig up your little extractor? Over."

"Depends. Older vehicles are better, less plastic in the way, no need for special tools. You can pull a battery while I'm doing that."

"Okay, give us a shout if you see anything. Over."

"There's a Supra coming up on the left, looks modified. We could check that?"

"The bright orange one? Over."

"What's left of it anyway."

The Unimog grunted to a stop and Ada hopped out onto the torn up surface of the M25, torch in hand.

"How's our patient doing?" She asked as Jack approached with his toolbox.

"Sleeping. You know, you should probably ask his name."

"I didn't want to push him. Besides, it doesn't really matter, does it?"

"What are you gonna tell this 'Chris' when we roll up?"

"We found someone who said they know him, but he's in too bad a shape to tell us much more. We tried our best to help him, but ultimately we're not doctors."

Jack pulled the bonnet pins off and laughed to himself as the hood sprung open. "Glad whoever owned this never worked on my car…" He lifted the dented panel clear and motioned for Ada to shine her torch inside. She gave the handle a few quick turns, then held it over his shoulder.

"Over here… Yeah, we're in luck. Let me just…" He pulled a small knife from his toolbox and scraped some plastic off the wires around the fuel pump. Next, he pulled a tangled mess of cables out and attached the clips to the freshly revealed wire. Tapping the other end against the battery produced a satisfying whirr.

"Alright, looks like we're in business. I'm gonna run it through to get rid of the petrol. Undo this battery… You wanna go get the jerry cans? A couple of vans around here we can run dry."

Ada nodded. "On it."

She returned a few minutes later, lugging three large metal fuel cans and a smaller red plastic one with a nozzle on top.

Jack had liberated the battery from the car and had even made a carrying strap out of the seatbelts.

"Very fancy," Ada said with a grin.

"It'll do."

"Any sign of the driver?"

Jack shook his head. "No. But judging from the damage, they were probably thrown clear. Look at the roof, this thing has rolled loads, and this belt wasn't being worn."

"Jesus…"

"Yeah, well let's not focus on that." He slung the battery over his shoulder, scooped up the pump and connected spaghetti of wires, then picked up his toolbox. "Saw a transit up against the barrier, we should start there."

When Jack went back to his van to drop off his tools, Ada checked in on the patient. To her relief, his breathing had evened out, and while his face occasionally contorted into one of pain, he remained asleep.

Ada watched with curious eyes as Jack went from van to van, opening the fuel caps and pushing the tube inside. Every so often he'd ask her to swap containers or disconnect the battery. It took a while, and both stunk of diesel by the end, but they'd got their fuel.

They filled their tanks, threw the extra into the back of the Unimog, then started off once more.

* * *

Ada yawned as the sun crested over the horizon. They'd been on the M25 all night, smashing a path through thousands of vehicles, carving a route to the A13.

The walkie-talkie crackled. "We want this turn-off. For Tilbury."

A twisted mess of metal stretched across the five lanes. It had several bent signs still attached, barely holding on, but still proudly displaying their information. The largest of the three read 'Dartford Crossing' and 'Gatwick.' The two smaller signs both had 'A13' written on them, but only one mentioned Tilbury.

Ada revved the Unimogs engine and ploughed through the gnarled framework, pushing it aside, clearing all five lanes as it turned side-on and slammed into the barrier.

She led them up the incline, following the slip-road allowed them to avoid the chaotic scrapyard piled up on the roundabout, and soon enough, they had ascended onto the A13.

"How far? Over."

"If the rest of the A-thirteen is like this, we should be at the turn-off for Brentwood soon. Then we follow it through Stanford-le-Hope towards the river. I'm gonna need to use the men's room soon though."

"Same. Anywhere to stop along here? Over."

"If you mean services, then not really. Besides, they probably won't be in great shape. Sorry, Ade, but we might have to do this one au naturale."

"Think you can hold it 'til we reach L.G? Over."

"No, and there's no guarantee they'll have facilities either. Or even let us use them."

Ada sighed. "Okay, I'll keep an eye out for somewhere to stop."

With a long yawn, Ada pulled up in a gap, shut the engine off, and then jumped out before disappearing into the woodland alongside the road. Most of the trees had fallen against the onslaught of the storm. Stumps were jagged or uprooted entirely, and the remains of the treetops had tangled into one another, blocking off any potential progress with an impenetrable wooden weave.

Ada returned to the vehicles a short time later, rubbing her hands with a wipe before pocketing it.

She approached the Transit and gently pulled the rear door open. Peering inside, she saw their patient still fast asleep.

"Anything new?" Jack asked as he hopped the barrier.

Ada shook her head, then quietly closed the door again. "Still breathing."

"All we can hope for, right?"

"Given our medical knowledge? I'd say so."

"Hey, I've been thinking…"

Ada rolled her eyes. "What?"

"I think we should wear the armour, and make sure we're armed, but not threatening."

"Armour, yes. Weapons? No. We don't want to give them any reason-"

"Listen to me, Ade, London Gateway is a huge place, and if his friends are occupying it, they've probably got numbers and are well-organized enough to survive this long. We can't take any chances, especially considering the haul we've got."

"You are way too paranoid-"

"I'm driving around with a stabbing victim in the back of my van, possibly one who killed two other people! You're not paranoid enough!"

"Ugh. Jesus, Jack, fine, whatever. I'm too tired to argue with you right now."

"Right. So I've got a scaffolding bar, you should take the knife."

"No way. You got something that won't fucking kill people?"

"Says the woman who was running about earlier with a broken bottle."

"The situation has changed."

"How?" Jack replied. "That was to deal with a threat. We could be driving straight into another one."

"Ugh! Just give me whatever! Need I remind you that he could be dying in there? And you're just standing around figuring out how we're gonna hurt more people."

"I don't want to hurt anyone!" Jack replied. "I just want to make sure *we* don't get hurt!"

"I already said do what you want."

Ada turned and hopped back into the Unimog, started the

engine, then started off down the clearer sections of road.

* * *

"This looks like the place," Jack said, handing the binoculars to Ada. The port was a scattered mess of fallen cranes and brightly coloured boxes. In the distance, she could clearly see several trucks driving from the port proper to a stretch of cleared concrete. Several hastily repaired cranes moved the containers they carried into a large circular formation.

"Looks like they're putting up a wall…"

Jack nodded. "Can you see how they're reinforcing it?"

Peering through the binoculars again, Ada followed the trucks to their drop-off point and watched as a container was unloaded. Her curiosity rose as a group of four heavily set men approached it with a long, wide tube before pressing it into the concrete. All four took hold of the device, one shouted something, then the tube made a bang loud enough for Ada to hear.

"Jesus! What the hell was that?" She asked, adjusting the focus.

"Looks like they're driving hooks into the ground."

As the four men staggered back, another small team stepped in and began tossing wire cable over the containers. The wall was too high and set up like brickwork. Ada watched as the new team pulled the wire through the hook and used a winch to tighten it. Another person stepped over and clamped the wire down tight, twice, then moved over to the next section.

"Oh!" Ada exclaimed. "That's pretty clever!"

"As long as the storm doesn't pull the hooks out, then sure. And judging from the suspension on those trucks, I'd say they're using the heavy containers for the bottom, and empty ones for the top."

"Is that wise?" Ada asked, lowering the binoculars.

"Well… If the system does fail, I guess I'd rather have an empty container fall on me than a full one. Neither option sounds too appealing though if I'm honest."

"If they continue the circle round, they're going to have a significant sized camp on their hands." She grinned. "Maybe we should join them!"

Jack raised his hands. "Woah, easy there, Ade. We don't even know if they're friendly yet."

"Oh, Christ, here we go again."

"I'm not saying it's a bad idea, I'm just saying we need more information."

"Okay, okay, fine." She looked out over the wall again. "So, how are we doing this?"

A few minutes later, Jack's Transit slowly rolled towards the opening in the containers at the end of the road.

"Jesus, Jack," Ada said, trying to get comfortable. "How do you live like this?"

"If you're talking about the mess, someone decided to fill up the back of my van with camping equipment. I didn't have anywhere else to put it."

"Okay, smart-arse. Hey, slow down will ya? We're trying to look as non-threatening as possible."

Jack's gaze fell on a small truck as it rolled through the entrance on a path directly towards them.

"Might be a bit late for that."

"Just be cool." She leaned over and jabbed the warning light button. The dashboard clicked, the indicator lights flashed.

"What'd you do that for?"

"Trying to interact with them. Better than honk-" She grinned. "Ha! Would you look at that."

The incoming truck had turned its hazard lights on in

response.

As the Transit rolled to a stop, Ada jumped out, empty hands out by her sides. "Hey!" She called out as several people emerged from the back of the truck. Jack exhaled so hard his breath fogged up part of the windscreen. He jumped out with his hand firmly wrapped around the knife handle.

"Help you?" A tanned, hollow-faced man asked, keeping his distance. His voice had an accent to it, but she couldn't place it.

"Not me," Ada replied. "We found one of your friends at Heathrow airport. He's in really bad shape, we tried to patch him up, but I haven't got any medical experience." She thumb-pointed to the van. "He's in the back, I can take you to him if you like?"

"How about you bring him out here?"

Ada could feel Jack tensing and raised her hands. "Okay, that sounds reasonable." She turned and headed for the rear doors, while Jack backed away slowly, keeping his eyes on the six-strong group ahead of him.

"Something doesn't feel right here, Ade."

"Yeah, it's all this testosterone in the air. Here, help me will you?"

Keeping one eye on the group, and another on Ada, Jack grabbed the stretcher and helped lower it onto the road before Ada jumped back down.

They carried him over to the hollow-faced man, whose stony expression disappeared as he laid eyes on their patient.

"Tim?" He dropped down beside him, the group closed in. "What the hell happened to you?"

"He shouldn't really talk," Ada said as Jack backed away. "We found him with a knife in his chest. Looked like he'd been in a fight. He'll need time to recover and a proper doctor."

"Fuckin' hell."

"He said Chris could help him?"

"Chris? He's the guy in charge." He looked up at Ada. "I'll take you to see him."

Jack frowned. "Why us?"

"Because..." The man replied as he motioned to the team to pick up the stretcher. "Tim and Chris are brothers. They're very close." He stood and offered Ada his hand. "Marco."

"Ada." She replied, shaking it. "You've got a nice accent, where you from?"

"Sardinia." He replied, extending the same hand to Jack.

"Picked a bad time for a holiday."

"Jack." He said, firmly shaking Marco's hand to another of Ada's eye-rolls.

"There seem to be a lot of people here." Ada continued. "More than we've found anywhere else."

"Most are from London. I survived in the underground. Others come from bunkers. Chris and Tim came from Churchill's war rooms. I think this is fitting." He motioned to the entrance. "We can talk more inside. Come."

Ada followed Jack back to the Transit and hopped up into the passenger seat.

"See?" She said as they pulled forward. "You get further in this world by helping people."

"Or we're driving into the Lion's den."

Ada sighed. "I swear, I don't know why I put up with your shit."

"It was your idea to team up."

"Yeah, before I knew you were such an argumentative, paranoid bastard."

"I'm being a realist," Jack replied. "It's the end of the world, Ade, people are going to loot and steal to survive, using any means necessary. If they find out we've got shit they could use-"

"What shit? Look around you. They're obviously going through everything here. We might have found a couple of packets of decent ready-to-eats, they're gonna be finding containers full. If anyone has a right to be suspicious, it's them."

They were greeted with curious stares from the relatively large group working tirelessly to assemble the outer barricade. Ada jumped at another loud 'pop'.

They came to a stop beside a cluster of disorganized containers near the back of the wall. Multi colored tarps flapped in the breeze, bridging the gaps between what appeared to be buildings.

The group in the truck hurried out, carrying Tim and the stretcher towards a container hidden in shade with a red cross crudely sprayed on the side.

Marco watched them, then headed inside another metal box. Ada and Jack sat in wary silence, observing the organized mayhem around them. Groups ran back and forth with tools and wires while trucks and cranes unloaded the containers into a set forty foot by forty foot square, all separated by pathways of concrete.

"Looks like more than just a survival camp." Ada finally said. "Looks like they're trying to build something more long-term here."

"Could be. I still don't fancy their chances if the storm arrives."

"Why not? Storm comes, you just hide in the containers with the doors shut, right? They're made to withstand the ocean aren't they?"

"I suppose so. Seeing how those hooks hold up will be the real key."

"Hey, here he is." Ada nodded towards Marco and the huge lumbering man behind him. "Jesus. Guess we know why he survived. The storm must have taken one look and been like 'fuck that'."

She opened the door and lowered herself onto the concrete with a smile. "Hi."

Chris spoke with a deep but soft voice. "I have the two of you to thank for Timothy's survival?"

"We got him this far, it's up to your people now."

"I have my best looking at him now. They believe that your

unorthodox methods may have saved his life."

Ada grinned. "Awesome!"

"My name is Chris, Chris Banks. And this is Container City."

He raised his hands to the surroundings. "I know, it isn't much

to look at now, but give it time. We'll make somewhere that

even the weather can't tear down."

"I'm Ada. This is Jack. We're like wandering scavengers I

guess."

Jack offered a stoic nod, remaining close to the van door.

"And the two of you were at Heathrow?"

She nodded. "Yep."

"Did you see anyone else?"

Her expression faded. "Um… yeah. Two others, both dead."

Chris' shoulders sank. "That is… unfortunate. I will send

someone out to collect our fallen."

Jack frowned. "Might wanna send more than two next time."

Chris glanced over at him with serious eyes atop a wry smile.

"It was never my intention to send anyone in the first place.

Timothy took it upon himself to seek out Heathrow Airport."

"Why?" Ada asked.

"He believed we should make use of the fresh food there

before it gets looted by others, or goes out of date. He also wondered if we should set up there instead." He started back towards the container buildings. Ada fell in behind Marco, and, after a reluctant sigh, Jack joined them.

"We've found some food in these containers, but when the main power went, we couldn't keep the reefer units going, so a lot of it went bad."

"Reefer units?" Ada asked.

"Oh. Please forgive me. They're refrigerated containers."

Jack frowned. "They haven't got built-in power sources?"

"Unfortunately not. With this in mind, Timothy took it upon himself to scout out other areas. The fighting in London means he had to go farther afield."

"Hold up," Ada replied. "Fighting?"

"Oh yes. It's quite bad. There are a lot of bunkers in London, and a fair number of underground train stations, but none of them were stocked with food or water. Flooding forced most people back to the surface. They fight one another for resources or space in the places that are holding up."

"So where does that leave you?" Jack asked.

"When the war rooms flooded, we had little choice but to abandon it. A tragedy that such a place will likely never recover." He exhaled. "As my family and I wandered, it occurred to me that there had to be a better solution. We came across some riverside construction, everything but the container had fallen into the water. That's when it hit me."

Ada grinned. "The container?"

"The potential solution. A place for us on the surface, not cowering underground like rats, oftentimes *with* rats, I hasten to add."

"So all this…" Ada replied, motioning around. "It can survive the storm?"

"We hope so. We're building low, reinforcing everything we can. We're driving stakes deep into the concrete, and screwing the containers down from the inside. If the storm can move that, then…" Chris blew the air out of his cheeks. "Frankly it can have it, it'll have earned it."

Jack grunted. "Quite a large team you got here."

"Other survivors from London who were sick of the fighting. We don't all see eye to eye, but I won't allow my leadership to be challenged. My vision is to provide somewhere safe for any survivor who is willing to work if they can't agree to work with me, they're welcome to return to London."

Ada nodded to Jack. "See, this guy gets it. Find a place, stake a claim, rebuild. Help others, but don't let them take the piss."

"Great." Jack exhaled. "Another 'embrace the apocalypse' type."

"Ha, no, Jack, you have me mistaken. My work here should prove that my intention is to return to a normal life. Roads, vehicles, buildings, production, luxury, security, and comfort, perhaps even scientific advancement for this new world. If we can establish what caused this storm, perhaps we can predict it, or better protect ourselves against it."

"Or reverse it," Ada added. "Right?"

"I am unwilling to make such promises, but if it's possible, and we're able, we'll do our best."

"What about food?" Jack asked. "You can't live off the containers forever."

"Perhaps not, but we can certainly live off them for some time. Long enough to establish other solutions."

Chris led them inside one of the containers and offered them one of several plastic seats lining the walls while he made a few short strides to the rear. He flicked on a strip of LEDs and sat down.

"Hey, look…" Jack started. "This is nice and all, but why are we here?"

Chris studied him with a perplexed frown. "I'm trying to be hospitable. You saved my brother's life."

"We could be anyone, aren't you wor-"

Ada raised her hands. "Jack, chill."

Chris relaxed back in his chair with a grin. "I know you're the sort of person who goes to the trouble of patching up someone who's been stabbed, then drives them all the way here, and so far neither of you have asked for fuel, or food, or any sort of reward for your trouble. That's the sort of people I believe you both to be. So, no, Jack, before you ask, I'm not worried. Good people find good people."

Ada sat down. "See? Just chill, already."

"You can stay here and make nice. I'll be in the van, sleeping."

"Oh come on…"

"No, Ade, you're on your own. You wanted to come here. We're here. I'm not doing anything more." He cast a sideways glance at Chris. "When you're done, you know where you can find me."

Ada watched as he disappeared from view, then let out a sigh. "Sorry about him."

"No need to apologise." Chris replied. "We've met plenty like him on our journey here. And in a way, he's right to be like that, but neither of you has anything to fear here. I give you my word that while inside these walls, you have our protection."

Ada wiped her face and nodded. "Thanks."

"What's the deal between the two of you anyway? I must admit, you make an interesting pairing."

"I was driving along, then bam, out of nowhere I see this guy waving his shirt around, warning lights flashing, the works. I pulled up, we got talking, the two of us have been scavenging together ever since."

"It doesn't seem like a harmonious relationship."

"To be honest? It isn't. He's an uptight arse who thinks any other survivors are out to rob or kill us."

"He isn't wrong. I offered help to the wrong people, and I paid the price. Timothy went out in an attempt to help us, and you saw where that landed him. Ask anyone here, they'll tell you a similar story. Your friend is right to think the way he does."

"If I listened to everything he said, I wouldn't be sitting here now. Tim would still be lying in Heathrow airport. And I'd be crawling around in some wrecked building while he stands around outside moaning."

"But that glint in your eye tells me you wouldn't want to do it alone."

Ada squinted at him. "No… I suppose I wouldn't."

"Everything in moderation, Ada. Let Jack's paranoia temper your desire to help and see the good in everyone, and the two of you will go far in this new world."

"I might not want to do it alone, but I don't know if I can keep doing it with him…"

Chris leaned forward. "The work the two of you do, you said you were scavengers?"

"Yeah… Jack hates the term, thinks it makes us sound like criminals. Prefers salvagers… Think I heard him use the words recovery experts once."

"Well whatever you call yourselves, you're obviously skilled enough to traverse these roads and bring wounded back home, so I have no reason to doubt your 'acquisition' abilities."

"Acquisitors! Jack'd love that."

Chris grinned. "So perhaps we can come to an agreement?"

Ada shrugged. "I'm listening."

"Jack is correct. We cannot survive on the containers alone. We don't know what's inside them until we open them, and despite our haste, we seem to be finding a lot of things that aren't edible. Not for a healthy diet anyway."

"Oh, really?"

"If we're going to establish ourselves here, we need to have many options for our food supply. Some days, we might recover a lot of food from the containers, but on the days we don't we'll need someone to find it elsewhere."

"And you want that someone to be me and Jack?"

Chris nodded. "At first. But then as you feel more comfortable here, perhaps you could train up others? Two scavengers won't keep us afloat if we hit a bad patch with the containers."

Ada exhaled. "I don't know, Chris. I'll have to speak to Jack."

He blinked. "Don't you want to know what we're willing to offer in return first?"

"Ah." She grinned. "I suppose that would help."

"This is why you need him, or someone like him. To temper your enthusiasm." Chris relaxed back again. "Once the houses are assembled, you'd be welcome to one each. I'm also happy to provide you both with meals, water, and a place to secure your vehicle. We use a similar hook and wire system for our trucks that we use for the buildings."

"Wait, wait." Ada raised her hands. "Let me get this straight.

You'd give us a house, *each*, free food, free water, and a parking space, and all we need to do is dig around some old ruins looking for the good loot?"

"That's the gist of it."

"Even if Jack doesn't agree to this, I'm totally in."

"Ah." Chris leaned forward. "As much as I admire your enthusiasm, I'm really only extending this offer to the both of you. You strike me as capable, but rash. If you're going to train people or go into these dangerous places, I need to know you're level-headed, and have someone capable of watching your back."

Ada's chest sunk as she exhaled. "And I suppose that person couldn't be one of your guys?"

"Timothy and Brandon were our self-proclaimed scavengers. One of them is dead and the other is being stitched up as we speak. I refuse to let that happen again, which it might if I send untrained people to join you. As you and Jack already have experience, already work together in a seemingly capable albeit difficult partnership, I am willing to offer you substantial incentives for working with us, but only if you do so together."

"Jesus." She exhaled. "I suppose I better go and talk to him then."

"I wish you luck," Chris replied. "You know how to get back to your vehicle?"

Ada opened her mouth to say something, then paused. "Uh. Yeah." She pointed. "That way, right?"

Chris nodded. "Right."

"Well… I'll let you know how it goes I guess."

"Indeed. And thank you again, Ada."

"Yeah, yeah…" She grumbled, stepping back outside. "Don't mention it."

Ada paused, then turned back to Chris. "Hey, I don't suppose you've found any welders?"

"A few, however, we lack the gas to operate them."

"Microwaves?"

"Honestly?" He replied with a smirk. "Thousands of the bloody things."

"I'm not making any promises, but my job might be easier if I had one."

Chris studied her with a confused glare, then nodded. "Very well, I'll have one brought over."

Ada stumbled back to the Transit, red-faced, carrying a heavy cardboard box by the handles. She rested it on the rear step, knocked on the back door, then saw Jack's head appearing through the passenger window.

"Ah, you've finished with King 'Kong'-trainer then?"

Ada grinned. "You're not jealous are you?"

"Think you're confusing me for somebody else."

"Can you come open the door? I've got a present for you."

"It's not another almost dead person, is it?" He asked, jumping out.

"No, but I can probably find you one if you like?"

"A microwave?" Jacked asked.

"Yeah. I asked if they had welders, but something, something, gas."

He nodded. "Makes sense. They'd probably be welding all these containers together if they could…"

He slid open the side door and took hold of the box. Ada quickly cleared enough space, then stepped back.

"All we need now is some batteries. I think I can get the thick cable off the trailer… maybe even run that as the power-"

"They've offered us a place here." Ada blurted. "Chris says if we scavenge for him, he'll give us a house each, parking spaces, food, clean water, the works. But, the offer only stands if *both* of us agree to it because he thinks I need you to 'temper my enthusiasm'."

Jack blinked.

"Personally I think it's a good deal, and Chris has already promised me that while we're here, we're under his protection. Eventually, he wants us to train up other scav- er... 'Extraction experts', so he needs us for the long-term. We still get to do our thing, we benefit from whatever they find in the containers here, and we can work on our trailer gardens whenever we're not working. And since there are so many hands here, they might even help us! Or vice versa, right? Like if the gardens are successful, maybe they can transplant the idea to containers? We could really do some good here, Jack."

He looked at her pleading eyes. His chest heaved as he inhaled. "And if I refuse, you lose out too?"

"From the sounds of it. He doesn't want me going out alone in case something happens, and we found his last two scavengers at the airport. Similarly, you can't go crawling through these places without me."

"But I'm no use to you if something does happen, am I? I can't follow you in and pull you out."

"No, but you can get a message back here, and I reckon with

all the trucks and many hands at their disposal, digging me out won't be too difficult." She raised her hands. "But I don't intend on it coming to that. You're right, Jack, I need to be more careful."

"You're just saying that-"

"No. Now that we've found this place? Now that I know for certain that there are other people out here, and they could use our help in exchange for somewhere I can live safely? I always wanted to survive, but now there's more purpose to it, right? If I want to see this place flourish, if I want us to do well, then I absolutely need to be more careful."

Jack turned away, glancing at the microwave, then back at Ada. "We get a house each?"

"Yeah. From the looks of it, it's two containers side by side, they reinforce them and cut doorways in to make rooms. I had a quick look while I was waiting for that to be delivered. They've made kitchens out of pallets… The bathroom is a bit simplistic, a water barrel, a couple of buckets, one of which has a toilet seat fitted to it." She shrugged. "Standard end-of-the-world composting toilet I guess."

"It's better than we've got…"

Ada nodded. "Anything is better than nothing, Jack."

He fixed her with a firm stare. "If we do this, and things get shady, or they start doing shit or ordering us to do shit that we don't like, then we're gone, okay?"

"We discuss it first. Your idea of shady might be a necessary evil in this new world."

"You're not convincing me, Ade."

"Okay, fine. If shit gets bad, we'll leave." She looked up at him. "Does that mean we're doing this?"

Jack exhaled. "Yeah, yeah. Alright."

Ada leaped up, almost knocking Jack to the ground with a hug. "Thank you!"

"Alright, easy, Ade."

She let go, then grinned. "I suppose we better go get Moggy."

"You should probably tell Chris first. It'll look weird if we just drive off."

She nodded. "Right. Be back in a sec'."

She turned, heading back towards the containers with a skip in her step and a smile on her face.

"This is it, Ada." She said to herself. "You get to be part of humanity's survival." Her smile grew. "Game on."

33089998R00139

Printed in Poland
by Amazon Fulfillment
Poland Sp. z o.o., Wrocław